DEDICATION

To the Mountains climbed, and the hitchhikers who traveled on the roads of no return, and to grandchildren who wonder who we were.

WHEN SOMEWHERE

IS NEVER ENOUGH

J.T. DODDS

Cover Pic Stephanie Greene- on unsplash

77 Rio Papaloapan
Ajijic, Jalisco, México 45920
Tel: 52 332 605 5432
jtdodds@hotmail.com

Sometimes life takes you on a pendulum's swing,
and when you end up on the other side of yesterday
you gotta go with the flow, or it's going to swing back
real fast, and leave you hanging.
– To Each Their Own Goodbye

.

The Farmers Daughter

ONE

On an unusually warm January morning, not a hint of breeze made it through the wide open double windows beside Luc Barbon's bed. His apartment, he called Hôtel Rouge, was long and narrow with sealed bay windows in the front room. Even if there was a breeze there was nowhere for it to go. He lay naked on top of the sheets, going over and over again in his mind the turn of events of last night. His expectation was the ride he was on was going to have a happy ending. It was what fairy tales were made of. Now, reality set in, and all that was left to hold onto was the aroma of flesh and sweat lingering on the sheets. His satiated body left him with a lack of kinetic interest in moving. He stared out over the postage stamp backyard's wooden fence, the two stained glass windows on the grey stone sidewall of St. Patrick's Cathedral muffled the sound of the Missa Cantata inside. In the window on the left side of the building St. Anthony, the patron saint of lost souls, lost lovers, and straying partners, with his arms full of flowers, cherubs, and books, was the perfect guy to hang outside his window. Luc could relate.

St. Cecilia, hanging out to Tony's left playing her harp, with little cherubs floating about, and an angel watching over her maidenhood, reminded Luc of early attempts at satisfying the elusive thing called love. Both saints were holding a lily indicating they were dead virgins, seemingly a criteria for saints earning a stained glass window. From Luc's perspective having an affair with Pam, was a lesson in love, and for her, well, he made her feel special. She told him that, and she told him she would slip out in the morning and let him sleep in. Neither one was capable of saying goodbye, even when they knew in their hearts it might probably be forever.

He was just beginning to feel sorry for himself when the Cathedral bells turned his thoughts into white noise. He grudgingly sat up leaned over and shut the windows ineptly muffling the sound. With the novelty of moving into his new apartment he had ignored the fact the back bedroom bordered onto the Catholic Cathedral. Besides the irritable antics of a Quasimodo, the whole Catholic quandary carried with it memories he would rather not resurrect. He climbed down from a bed that took up three quarters of the room. He walked down the narrow hallway peering into the rooms to his left, bathroom, next the galley kitchen, and entered the living room, in his mind half expecting to find her. In the front room he leaned over his desk and stared out the bay windows, searching for something he knew he'd lost, without hope, or a promise of ever finding it again. One floor below him the street was empty, her Bonneville was gone, and it scared him. In a short period of time he'd come a long way from nowhere, and he was in no man's land again, having just stepped off a train onto an empty platform, into somewhere he had no past, and an unknown future.

Luc shook off yesterday under a hot shower. Put on a clean t-shirt and his Levi cutoffs, tied up his red converse all stars, scrambled a couple eggs, and wrapped them in

3

warm tortillas. After cleaning up he grabbed his canvas leather messenger shoulder bag Pam had given him, and was down the stairs and out the door. Standing on the sidewalk, Stanton Street was busy with morning commuters, the weather in the lower 50s, briskly climbing toward the mid-sixties, typical for January in El Paso, Sun City Texas. He was not so much in hurry as he was in anticipation of his destination. He was half way through and about to start the final leg, notwithstanding a twist of fate, of what so far over the last couple years had been the proverbial good, bad and ugly.

TWO

It was the morning of his first day enrolled at the University of Texas El Paso. His immediate task was to stop in at the registrar's office to pick up his photo ID, and meal card. Having performed the mundane task of semester registration three times previously at other institutions he could walk through it blinded folded. The young women behind the counter had her back to him, searching in a file cabinet.

"Good morning miss," he said, as he leaned over the counter to get a better look.

"Be right with you," she responded, without turning around. "Just need to finish up here."

Luc didn't mind the wait. It reminded him of another time and another place where an interest in the girl behind the counter took him for an unexpected ride. From his viewpoint her jeans were a perfect fit. When she turned around, if he thought there was not much room for improvement, he was wrong. Her long, golden blonde curls matched his own head of hair in length. In an environment where 85 percent of the population were brown skinned, her face was a pale white, making the blue eyes and pink lips all the more pronounced. Kate was the name on her name tag.

"Hi Kate, I'm here to pick up a meal card." He could not help staring.

"And you are?" she said, cracking a smile, that acknowledge his attention.

"Right! Luc, Luc Barbon." He unfolded his letter of acceptance and handed it to her.

"Well, welcome Luc. Let me get your file." She dipped around, opened a drawer in the cabinet, and selected a folder. He followed her every move. She retrieved his card, and in the file noticed the last school he went to.

"Do you know Albert Hogan?" she asked, handing him the meal card.

"Albert? Yes, he's my best friend. Actually, he's my only friend in El Paso. We last attended Big Bend State together." He looked at her name again, and made the connection. "Kate DeVry. Are you...Albert's girlfriend?" He couldn't pull it together to say fiancé.

"The one and only, I think." Now the smile was permanent. "He's told me about you Luc. I should have recognized the name from when Albert filed your paperwork."

"Good things I hope."

"Nothing but the best. I see you live on North Stanton near the Cathedral. I live in Hotel Dieu adjacent to the church. It's a residential school for nurses. We're practically neighbors."

"And you're attending UTEP as well as the nursing school?"

"Only for the Academic courses Hotel Dieu doesn't offer. Plus I work part time here. It gives me spending money and most importantly gets me out of the dorm. The nun's run the place like a convent."

"If it's the building adjacent to the church, and you need to escape anytime we're only a fence apart. I mean, if

Albert doesn't mind, that is. He hasn't dropped by to see me yet. You're more than welcome though."

He had invited her to his apartment without thinking. It just slipped out. He tried to backtrack, then decided to stop talking while he was behind.

"Thanks for the invitation. I haven't climbed a fence since I left the farm. I haven't seen a lot of Albert lately either, he's bogged down with his politics on and on off campus." She put his letter in the file. "Is there anything else you need?"

"Not at the moment. I guess I'll see you around campus."

"Maybe some Sunday after mass?" Kate returned to the cabinet.

The rest of the day was tying up loose ends around his class schedule with the English Department, and checking out the location of his classes that would begin tomorrow. Luc's Liberal Arts schedule included courses in Creative Writing and Drama and the usual mandatory credits. Obtaining a map he wandered about the campus that had been around since 1917, orienting himself to the lay of the land. At times he felt like being in the orient. His overseas assignment in the Army was in Thailand close to the fighting in Vietnam. The campus architect was a modern version of 17th century Bhutanese. He could have been in the Himalayas. He had lunch in the cafeteria with his new meal card and returned to Hôtel Rouge. Back at the apartment curiosity got the best of him and he checked his bedroom window's view of Kate's dorm. Luc thought about what had transpired earlier in the day. He had not touched base with Albert since his initial meeting at the Kentucky Club in Juarez when he first arrived with Pam. Coincidently meeting up with Albert's girlfriend and her stopping in on a Sunday morning, he didn't see any problem with that.

Luc's schedule facilitated his penchant for avoidance, and maintained his status quo of being invisible around crowds. Getting involved seemed to be his quagmire, and he was determined, this time around to keep his distance from whatever, or whomever, might derail his quest. Not living on campus his meal ticket was less than useless. On Monday, Wednesday, and Thursday, he was lucky to make it to his 8 A.M. class let alone arrive on campus in time for breakfast, and with classes running through 1:20 P.M. he either skipped or missed lunch. Craving sustenance, and given his limited income, his only option was stopping at the Rio Grande Bar and Grill on Stanton Street. It became an unavoidable temptation on his walk home. He loved eight ball, and around the table at the Bar and Grill there was always someone hungry for a challenge to their manhood and wallet. Rack-em, was music to his ears, and his ability to run the table, fine-tuned during his military service for lack of other recreational activities, usually paid for some snacks from the bar, if not very healthy, curbing his need for sustenance.

On Tuesday and Thursday, with one class mid-morning, and one mid-afternoon he had hours of on campus downtime. It was his opportunity to use his meal card for a decent breakfast and a lunch that came with an unexpected bonus. Kate worked the registrar's office part-time on Monday, Tuesday and Thursday and made Luc's intolerable schedule tolerable by joining him occasionally during lunch hour. Through the month of January, Albert was still MIA and Kate was the only person Luc socialized with outside of the Rio Grande Bar and Grill. She was definitely an improvement over hanging around a pool table. Vibrant, talkative, and well informed of the campus comings and goings, she was also skilled at languages and had studied Spanish in high school. Once she discovered Luc was a Francophone, from Ontario, Canada, who joined the U.S. Army, she got to practice her French. She grew up on a farm near Columbia, Missouri, and if the Ozarks were like living on another planet, her description of life in Missouri was right there floating around the universe with it. Luc looked forward to the all too infrequent visits with Kate, even more when they extended to an occasional rendezvous on the sandy knoll behind the Administration building she worked in.

THREE

The sandy knoll was a quiet, seldom occupied space where Luc found retreat from the campus hustle while tackling the heavy reading requirements of a junior in the English Department. Kate, on break, joined him on the last day of January. She sat cross-legged on the ground beside him. Grass was at a premium in Southwest Texas.

"Didn't expect to find you here Luc, on a Monday afternoon. Pleasant surprise."

"The eagle shit today. I don't have to hustle lunch at the bar.

"Didn't know you're into bird watching."

"Not exactly. GI Bill. Its payday. I'm waiting for the check to arrive at the campus post office."

He put his copy of Henry James *Portrait of a Lady* down. Not without some relief, for the author's sentences, the length of a normal paragraph were a challenge to read.

"I told Albert you often stop for lunch at the Rio Grande. He says he wants to meet up with you. He's been very busy with campus life, and his politicking. I only get

WHEN SOMEWHERE IS NEVER ENOUGH

to see him when it's a social thing. You'd never know
we're getting married."

"Right, I almost forgot you were getting, hitched I
believe is the word for it in Texas.

He was joking of course. Luc didn't forget.
Marriage was a subject they didn't touch on. Kate was a
free spirit and saw no need to complicate her relationship
with Luc. She too enjoyed these little get-togethers. He was
different than Albert in ways she never experienced with a
man. He paid attention to her without demanding anything
in return. She uncurled her legs and lay back, putting her
hands behind her head she stared at a cloudless sky. She
couldn't remember when it last rained. Living in the
Southwest desert was a long way from Missouri. She had
broached her upcoming marriage and continued with the
topic.

"It won't be long now, and of course you'll be
invited to the party. Twenty days from today to be exact,
until the big day."

"You don't have to worry then about it raining on
your parade. You having a big reception, church wedding
and all?"

"No. Albert's arranged for a Justice of the Peace.
He wants something simple. We can't even go on a
honeymoon, what with our class schedules. My courses on
campus, and at the nursing school, will keep me busy
through summer. On top of that I have clinical sessions in
the evenings and sometimes on weekends at the hospital."

"When do you guys have time to get together let
alone time to get married?"

She rolled over on her side to face him. "This
semester it's been few and far between. I see you more than
I see him. I'm not complaining mind you. He was attending
Big Ben State when I first met him. I just finished my
sophomore year and was taking a required summer course
in civics. Albert was home for the break and was auditing

the class. You know he used to live here."

"I know his father was in the army, stationed at Fort Bliss."

"He hates his father, and was glad when he got sent to Vietnam."

She rolled back over and lay on her back. Luc reached over and tucked his backpack under her head.

"Those times were fun. It was easier for me to sneak out of the dorm back then. The nuns are excruciatingly more demanding with graduation on the horizon."

The Catholic cross to bear was something Luc had in common with Kate. They both had a history which continued to complicate their lives, and talked about parallel events under the papal thumb having impacted their formative years. Kate's dorm was a nunnery with strict rules of compliance and guilt. Her parents, Missouri farmers, enrolled her in Hotel Dieu Nursing School assured she would be safe from temptation under the ever present watch of Jesus on the cross and the omnipresent Sisters of Charity ever vigilant from under their habits. Albert was godless, in as much as he didn't know what the inside of a Catholic, or any denominational church looked like, with no intention of ever improving on that knowledge, unless his career goal as a politician might require him to play the game.

"Where do you plan to live?"

"That's another problem. There's no way I can move out of the dorm at Hotel Dieu until I graduate this summer. It's all part and parcel of the program I'm taking, and my folks are paying for. The nuns won't know I'm married. If they find out—well, we'll just have to deal with it."

"I see where it could be a problem. You'd be a bad influence on all the other Catholic girls. What about your folks?"

"They'd freak if they knew, and will probably disown me anyway for marrying a non-Catholic. I'm waiting until I receive my nursing certificate. I plan on telling them after the graduation ceremony."

Luc thought this was a 'what can go wrong' narrative, and he let what he considered Kate's rebellion alone. She was a natural beauty, the sun shining through her hair braided by the wind, the laughter in her blue eyes and a smile wrapped in alluring lips. She was soft, not a hard line about her, all curve, all there for the hungry eye, a feast for his male senses, and yet, on the road to marriage to Albert, untouchable. As she lay on the lawn, she brought forward another time, another place in his memory box, and it stimulated him—not necessarily in the brain. He lay back, cool sun warm on his face, it all felt good just being there.

"So you'll be together but living apart." He was talking to a small wisp of cloud overhead. "Why not wait until you're finished, and Albert has graduated as well."

Kate sat up, and looked at her watch. This was a sore spot with her. She wanted to wait but Albert insisted, even though it complicated things. Marriage was her only opportunity to break the bonds of parental and non-secular control, and waiting until she was on the brink of no return had its disadvantages. He might change his mind. She left it there. She didn't say why he didn't want to wait. Her break was up, and she needed to return to the registrar's office.

"I hope we can continue with our little rendezvous if you don't have any qualms about hanging out with a married woman. I really enjoy our time together."

She leaned over and kissed him lightly on the cheek, and headed down the knoll. He sat up and watched her walk away, and enter the Admin building. He didn't tell her he was probably still married, and obviously Albert hadn't relayed the story.

FOUR

"Well look who the armadillo dragged in. How's it going Albert?"

"Couldn't be better. Kate told me you hung out at the Rio Grande. Passing by, thought I'd check up on you."

Luc laid his pool cue on the green felt. He just ran the pool table, and his unlucky opponent was at the bar anteing up with a draft beer, and a bag of pretzels. He walked around the table and gave Albert one of those manly hugs where you combine a handshake with rubbing shoulders. He wasn't sure if hugs were appropriate in a West Texas bar. Albert, as always was dressed like a politician, white shirt and tie, sport coat, and black wing tip oxfords. In contrast Luc wore his uniform: tee-shirt, Levi's, and he took lately to wearing his scuffed up Justins. Levi cutoffs were his preference but not after seeing he was the only one campus in summer attire he felt a little self-conscious. Summer meaning spring through fall.

"Still dressing like a politician I see. Want me to rack-em?"

"Not today, on a tight schedule. I didn't know you were a hustler Luc. If I'd known we could have kicked some gaucho butt in the bars in Alpine. Could have made some mean money if you weren't so preoccupied screwing all the cowgirls. Did you ever see the movie The Hustler with Jackie Gleason as Minnesota Fats, and Paul Newman as "Fast" Eddie?"

"Great movie, but I'm not in the same league. It's not on my resume but pays for the occasional lunch. One of the few transferable skills I learned in the Army. Are you on your way somewhere? Got time for a beer at least?"

Albert check his watch. "I've got time for one."

"Good, let's grab a seat at the bar, we've got some catching up to do. They've got great nachos here, if you like jalapenos.

"Sounds good."

The Rio Grande Bar and Grill was your typical Texas watering hole; long wooden bar, in front of a wall lined with bottles of alcohol, small, round wooden tables with well-worn chairs, a plethora of pictures of people nobody knew anymore, along with plaques of Texas shitkicker sayings, and the obligatory good lookin' well-endowed bartender to keep the cowboys sucking on suds. Sunlight was optional. As soon as he pulled up a stool, Albert waved over the bartender who was leaning on the far end of the bar conversing with a customer.

"She's something elsc. What's her name?"

"Ginger. She's engaged to a trucker."

"Never an obstacle."

When she came over she gave Albert the onceover. He was a little upscale compared to her normal patrons.

"What'll it be Luc, I gather your friend's not playing for pretzels." She liked Luc, he was a gentleman compared to the rest of the broncos.

"Thought we'd have a look at the menu."

She laughed. "Same as always Luc, me or the nachos."

Albert played the gallant.

"Ginger honey, how about a large order of nachos, and whatever Luc's drinking, I'll have the same."

"We've only got Lone Star on draft, straight out of the Rio Grande."

Albert eyeballed her as she swayed back down the bar, and put in her order through a narrow window leading to the kitchen.

Luc waited until Albert came back down to earth and diverted his attention from Ginger.

"They only serve pickled eggs, pig skins, pretzels, and nachos until the cook gets out of bed and rolls in for the after work crowd. That usually runs until two in the morning."

"Too bad she's not really on the menu." He turned back to Luc. "Sorry I haven't been in touch. Since transferring here it's been non-stop involvement with school and community. Now with the wedding coming up, one more issue on the plate. How's the apartment, and your lady friend Pam. We're having a quiet wedding. You are going to bring her to our reception I hope."

"Pam decided to sell the ranch in Alpine, and move to San Antonio. I won't be seeing much of her."

"Sorry to hear it. Anyway you are coming? It'll be one hell of a party."

"Kate tells me you're getting married on President's Day weekend."

"Reception's on Friday at my place. I live in a small apartment complex off West Stanton Street, complete with a pool and common area. Walking distance from here actually. It's occupied by students, and a few working girls who like students. We have a regular Friday night BYOB get-together with an ample supply of outlaws and co-eds. You're invited any time. Just bring you're bathing suit—or not, no one's fussy about appearances. It's like living in a frat house, but without the gender limitations. My scholarship and student loans, plus a stipend make it all affordable."

This was a side of Albert that didn't manifest itself at Big Bend State. Luc's new impression was it's all about him.

"Kate tells me you won't be living together until after she graduates. Got to be tough."

"With Kate living in Hotel Dieu Dorm under the watchful eyes of the Sisters of Charity it has drastically curtailed quality time together. She's been able to escape on weekends sneaking out of the dorm. Few and far between now with the pressures of graduation. We'll be getting married on President's Day weekend, and the nun's think she's going on a school trip to visit the Texas Capital and Legislative building in Austin. After it'll be catch-as-catch-can until she graduates."

"What happens then?"

"She'll be working as a nurse bringing in an income, while I work on my Masters. Works for me."

When Ginger delivered the Nachos Albert struck up a conversation with her. He knew all the right lines, and knew how to charm the ladies. If he wasn't getting married in a couple weeks he would have gotten her phone number, and the days her fiancé was heading to Wyoming with his eighteen wheeler. When she broke up the conversation to serve other patrons, he leaned over to catch a glimpse of her ass as she walked away.

"She's something else. I can see why you hang out here." He took a nacho from the pile, bit down, and drowned it with beer. "Jeesuz, the jalapenos are hot!"

After eating a few more nachos, each followed by a slug of brew, he checked his watch. After one last look down the bar at ginger he disembarked from the bar stool.

"Look I gotta run. I have a part time job in the Mayor's office. I get a stipend, and I get extra credit for community service. It's a good gig. He pulled a card from his jacket pocket and handed it to Luc. "Here's my phone number. Let's not be strangers Luc, and don't forget about my Friday night get down and get dirty at the complex. You've got an open invitation. Oh Yeh, and the reception. It'll be at the apartment. No gifts, just come as you are. He laid down a fin to pay the tab. "Tell the sweet thang behind the bar to keep the change."

Albert was out the door leaving Luc still sitting on the bar stool. He didn't have a chance to thank him for the nachos, or let him know he didn't have a phone, let alone a watch. This was not the Albert he remembered sharing a semester with in Big Bend country, and not a man he could imagine Kate marrying. He was however someone on the way to becoming a politician.

Luc's lone wolf persona began to wear thin by mid-February, and the entertainment value of shooting pool for beers and bar food grew tiresome with the lack of competition. The Rio Grande Bar lost some of its charm when Ginger married her good buddy, and took off to Wisconsin in his rig. In keeping with his mildly depressing present outlook on life he buried his head in the writings of Charles Bukowski, Henry Miller, Kazantzakis, and D. H. Lawrence whose voluntary exile or "savage pilgrimage" as he called it, Luc could relate to. Luc's history was one of reclusiveness. His problem was he lacked the social impulse to join, and that was the prerequisite for an active campus life.

FIVE

Following their last rendezvous Kate was nowhere to be found on campus. He even got brave enough to casually peek in at the registrar's office a few times. When he first met Kate while registering for classes, she mentioned she might drop over some Sunday after the schools mandatory attendance at Sunday mass. He could see the dorm out his bedroom window, and fantasized her knocking on the door. That never materialized other than in his head. Now, on the pre-nuptial day before he figured Kate would be out of his life before she was in it, he headed for Albert's Friday night reception carrying a bottle of Tequila Sauza and a six pack. He wore his one and only jacket over his t-shirt figuring it might be a formal affair.

Luc followed the music of Three Dog Night into the middle of a smoke filled two bedroom apartment crowded with a couple dozen gyrating bodies moving in and out of the room like characters on an M.C. Escher canvas. It was anything but formal. He spotted an animated Albert, not wearing a tie, in conversation by glass doors leading out to what he could tell to be the pool area. Then he located Kate, sitting on a stool, in front of a counter separating the kitchen from the living room. Their eyes met and she waved him over. When he made it through the maze of bodies she jumped down off the stool and gave him a peck on the cheek. On impulse he glanced over the crowd to see if Albert was watching.

"Albert mentioned he met up with you. I was hoping you would show up. I missed seeing you on campus over the last couple weeks."

Kate took his Tequila and beer and moved around to the other side of the counter. He followed her. She was wearing the same tight jeans, and button busting western shirt that left nothing to the imagination she wore when he first met her. An innocent farmer's daughter he thought, wrapped in a cowboy's delight.

"Couldn't miss the reception for the only two friends I have in El Paso. It's a good thing I didn't wear my tux."

"These beers are warm, help yourself to a cold one on ice in the kitchen sink and throw these in." She held up the bottle of Sauza. "Unless you want to start with tequila."

"Beers fine. For now."

Beer in hand he joined her at the back of the counter. The kitchen area was a step up from the living room allowing them a view over the heads of the partygoers. She was also drinking beer and raised hers in a toast.

"Salud! You don't really have a tux, do you?"

"I've never worn one, then again I can't remember the last wedding reception I went to. This is a wedding reception, right? I thought I was going to be early." Luc scanned the room. "Looks like the parties in full throttle."

"It's not really a reception, which usually comes after the wedding, but were keeping everything low key this weekend. This is kind of a bachelor and bachelorette party all in one. Generally Albert's Friday night shindigs get started around sunset, this time it was noon, and it'll probably go on all night."

"Well, it's a special occasion."

"Not only that, since I have to be back at the dorm by eleven Albert decided to start the celebration early, and has been at it since probably this morning."

"Once you're married will you still have this curfew?"

"Until I graduate, but not this weekend. It's a three day holiday for Presidents' Day. I'm supposed to be on a student excursion to Austin tomorrow."

"He mentioned the trip when I met up with him at the Rio Grande Bar. As the student rep he was pretty slick at working deals during his time at Big Bend State. Are you looking forward to being married to a budding politician?"

On the far side of the room, Albert, surrounded by several people, was in a what looked like a heavy-duty conversation.

"Don't know, never met a politician before. I suppose I'm going to have to get used to crowds. It's my event, but you, Albert, and his roommate Steve, are the only ones I really know here. You'll meet Steve, he's classic."

When Albert broke free from his circle of friends and began making his way to the counter, Luc moved over to the sink to get another beer. Lone Star was like drinking water.

"Luc, you made it. Grab me one of those would you."

Albert stepped behind the counter and put his arms around Kate's waist. He noticed the bottle of tequila.

"Keep the bottle of Sauza handy Hon. Little known fact about this guy, he can more than match anyone drink for drink with tequila. I'm going to steal him away from you and introduce him to my compadres. Besides, if I didn't know he was a married man I wouldn't let him near my woman for any length of time."

As she watched them pinball back across the room she wondered how during registration she missed his being married. She resumed her seat on the stool and watched as they disappeared into one of the bedrooms. Married was a bit of a surprise and piqued her curiosity. There's more to this man, she mused. She was content to be Albert's bride-to-be, and sit and smile as the mostly unfamiliar male partiers stumbled up to the kitchen to get their drinks, complimenting her on how beautiful she was, and disappearing back into the milieu. There were several women in the apartment and out on the adjacent community pool area, none of whom Kate knew outside of a casual acquaintance. She was not having a bridal shower, and none of her friends in Hotel Dieu, with the exception of her roommate, had any idea she was getting married. She was a stranger in the room. It was something growing up as a single child on farm, and being a wall flower in high school prepared her for. Beside Catholicism, another thing she had in common with Luc.

Albert closed the bedroom door behind him, and with Luc in tow, walked up to two guys sitting on the edge of the bed sharing a joint. He put his arm around Luc's shoulder and introduced him.

"Like you to meet my buddy from Big Bend State via Canada. Luc meet the one and only Steve White, roommate and future Texas Attorney General. And the scary looking amigo is Angel, the only man you want to know on the border if you want to get stoned."

They both acknowledged Luc's presence, and Steve passed the joint he was smoking to Albert. To some in the Political Science Department Steve White, an outspoken senior, was an obnoxious son of a bitch, with all the attributes of a highly polished Texas lawyer, and he looked the part. He was tall, thin, and dressed like the Marlboro man from the Stetson to his black Hornback Alligator boots.

Ángelo Martinez Rivera's handle was Angel. He was not the spitting image of Cheech, of Cheech and Chong fame, but he could have passed for a double with his shoulder length curly jet black hair, horseshoe mustache resembling mini-ape hanger handlebars, and a perpetual smirk under a toque, as if he just pinched your wife's ass. He was the friendliest drug dealer in the Pass, and had the university market cornered. He was also one of the first enrollments in Chicano Studies at UTEP aiming for a B.A. Steve and Angel were trying to top each other on reciting the most ludicrous laws in Texas.

"Angel, just because he's been one step ahead of the law since he waded across the Rio Grande, thinks he's an encyclopedia of Texas jurisprudence. Impossible as it seems he's been challenging me to a dual of legal absurdities." It was Steve's turn.

"The Texas constitution, written over a bottle of whiskey and in the arms of a prostitute, states no religious test shall ever be required as a qualification to any office in this State; nor shall anyone be excluded from holding office on account of his religious sentiments, provided," Steve paused here for effect, "He acknowledges the existence of a Supreme Being."

Albert passed the number to Luc who didn't hesitate. He hadn't smoked pot since leaving Alpine.

"Good one Steve. I've got one for Angel who I'm sure has broken this law, maybe a couple times; in Texas it's legal for a chicken to have sex with you, but it's illegal to reciprocate."

Not to be bested by Albert, Angel retaliated.

"Watch your step cabrón; in Texas I can legally kill you as long as I tell you when and how I'm going to do it."

They all drank to the conundrum. Albert turned to Luc. How about something from the frozen north?"

"It's been a long time since I was in beaver country, but I think it's against the law to make burgers out of polar bears. I guess it wouldn't fly in Texas where you guys can shoot and eat anything, or anybody, and do."

He choked inhaling the last of the roach. Angel lit another joint.

Luc continued. "How about it's illegal to have sex with a domestic animal in Canada unless there are at least 3 males over 18 present and engaged in the activity."

Steve piped in, "Where did you find this guy Albert? I think we have a quorum here, and I do believe there are a few domestic animals out by the pool. First let's give your friend here a Texas welcome."

It was a lifetime ago in Dallas when he last snorted a line a line of coke, and it was easy to slip right back into it, especially with quality blow.

SIX

When it came time for Kate to head back to her dorm before her curfew, Albert, since for him the party was just beginning, jumped on Luc's offer to escort his bride-to-be home. By nine o'clock Luc was ready to split anyway, the only person he really wanted to talk to was leaving. He took full advantage of pretending to be Sir Walter Raleigh. Kate feigned disappointment at having to leave. No one seemed to take notice.

For the half dozen blocks it was a quiet walk downhill on Stanton Street. Luc was shaking off his reintroduction to the combination of drugs and booze, Kate, was content with the quarter moon, empty streets, and not having to think about anything but the moment. When she revealed it was an hour and a half before reporting in at the dorm he suggested maybe she'd like to stop off at his apartment for a glass of wine. It was tempting, she was caught between wanting to, and remembering she was getting married in the morning.

"It's a nice night, let's go around the corner and sit on the steps of the Cathedral."

Not as cozy as his apartment, but he wasn't complaining. They climbed to the top of the stairs. Luc took his jacket off and put it down for her to sit on.

"Did you enjoy yourself tonight Luc? You disappeared for quite a while after Albert kidnapped you."

"I must admit Albert's friends are captivating. Steve is quite the character. Fits the role of a Texas lawyer like Albert does the politician. I like Angel, but he can be dangerous with his unlimited access to drugs. I didn't see you out there mingling with the masses. I would think this was a big moment for you, last chance to let loose before tying the knot."

"To be honest I'm overwhelmed by large crowds. I know they're all just students, and it's what students do, get a little crazy, and Texas crazy, in Missouri where I grew up, is referred to as insanity.

"Well, for one, with his roommate off to school in East Texas things should quiet down."

"I'm hoping once we're married, and Albert is working on his Masters, things will settle down." Her voice didn't sound convincing.

"Are you looking forward to being married?"

Kate hesitated before answering the question.

"I thought it was a great idea when we made the decision. Albert was transferring to UTEP, and I so not wanted to go back to Missouri. You don't know what it's like to be a country Catholic. My life was dominated by nuns, priests, and parents who made my High School years seem like I was following the Stations of the Cross. They wanted me to join a convent. With the help of an elderly priest, who I'm sure got off on my confessionals, as mundane and repetitive as they were, I convinced my doubting Thomas parents Hotel Dieu and the Sisters of Charity would be a safe haven for my chastity, and nursing would equally serve the Father, Son, and Holy Ghost."

The top steps of the Cathedral were high enough to overlook the city, and as far as the eye could see it was awash in a silent bluish-green from the mercury vapor streetlights. Kate was lost in thought for the moment, then continued, but lowered her voice to just above a whisper considering she was on God's doorstep.

"In reality El Paso was as far away from home as I could get. Catholicism, once it has a hold of you, it doesn't want to let go."

Skill, drive, intelligence had little room to play out to their fullest where the social and financial opportunity did not present itself, and the cards were stacked against a woman. Too often there was no deck to play with. Kate, raised on a farm, in an orthodox religious environment, in the middle of a State which prided itself on white, male supremacy, she was given the options of convent, nursing, secretary, or married to someone who met the approval of the authorities dominating her life. She was reaching for something better.

"Any regrets?"

"For leaving Missouri, no. From jumping into marriage. Not yet."

She could feel the desert night drop in temperature and inched closer to Luc.

Luc's High School experience in an all-boys Catholic school taught by Benedictines, and Jesuits was the Way of the Cross rolled into a couple painful years before he escaped across the border. He could relate to her need to get out from under the dogma. She told him she skipped grades and graduated High School when she turned 17. Hotel Dieu, because of her grades, and St. Cecilia qualities, made an exception by admitting her at an early age, now in her early twenties she was graduating with honors. Luc found her bright, insightful, and a bit naïve if she thought riding off in Albert's pumpkin carriage was going to put her out of her Missouri, or Misery as it sounded like to him.

"I'm not exactly a role model, but sometimes marriage works out."

"Sometimes?" Luc felt a tinge of Déjà vu.

She decided to broach a subject she'd been curious about since Albert brought it up.

"Albert said you're married. Any regrets there?"

"It's a long story."

"I've got an hour before I turn into a pumpkin, can you make it a short story?"

Desert cold has a chill factor all its own as with marriage, which has nothing to do with Fahrenheit or Celsius. She edged up to Luc to where his body heat closed the gap between them.

"The story isn't any longer than yesterday. I was a bit naïve about the consequences of marriage. Do you know much about the rodeo town of Alpine that Albert and I lived in?"

"Only that it was four hours away, somewhere near Big Bend National Park. He told me there were nothing but cowboys there."

"And cowgirls. Allison's her name. She was born and raised in Alpine, and attending Big Bend State. Unmarried meant women had to live in the dorm. She hated it. Allison was a senior in the English Department. Into everything. We did a play together, a Moliere farce. She worked with Albert and me on the school paper. She's a delight, and sharp as a tack. The short and scary of it is, at a party we decided to get married. It was a business arrangement."

Luc could feel Kate stiffen.

"Are you getting cold? Do you want me to run over to the apartment and get something?"

"No, I'm okay. You're mister warm body. Your story is too close for comfort. Albert and I decided to get married at a party."

He stood up. Don't go away, I'll be right back. He returned in minutes from the apartment with a serape, and wrapped it around both of them. He put his arm around her shoulders. She squeezed in and eliminated any space between them.

"I spent months in the desert in Big Bend. It may be in the forties, but when you have a big drop in temp from day to night it feels a whole lot colder."

There was no resistance on Kate's part and once the chill was off, Luc continued with his story.

"Do you know anything about divorce in Texas?"

"No. It never entered my mind. I thought looking into divorce came after someone got married."

"Well, I never could draw a straight line. You can get a divorce in Texas simply by agreeing to get one. Something like getting married simply by saying you're married."

"I don't know if it's truth or fiction but I think Arab men can get a divorce by saying it three times to their wives."

"If it's true, Texas has more than just oil in common with them. Anyway, we thought getting married would get her out of the dorm, and I would almost double my GI Bill, and live high on the hog. At the end of the school year, we'd get a quickie divorce for around fifty bucks. It would be a marriage in name only, and both of us agreed to it."

"Obviously it didn't work out as expected or you wouldn't still be married." Kate found the story a little humorous.

"I'm not sure I'm still married. The papers were filed, hopefully, Allison may have followed through with the divorce after all. At any rate, as you have probably figured out it wasn't a marriage made in heaven. Allison came to the conclusion she didn't want to end the marriage. I hope I'm not being presumptuous here, in retrospect it seems similar to your wanting to escape from the confines of your environment. Allison got a glimpse of the outside world. A potential, in a rodeo dominated world, to escape the corral."

"What prevented you from getting involved with Allison? Could you not see yourself married and settling down on a ranch?"

"I told her I'm like a tumbleweed, when it matures and dries it cuts loose from its roots, and it tumbles away in the wind. Whether the divorce went through, I suppose I'll find out some day."

Being the night of the new moon, they were invisible in a shroud of darkness on the Cathedral stairs. Above them a porous sky of starlight that reminded Luc of Big Bend Country, and below the city spread out before them in a speckled serape. There was nothing more to say about tomorrow, and enough said about where life brought them to a point, as in the song "Stairway to Heaven," their stairway lay on the whispering wind. They huddled under the serape in silence, not from the chill, but from the unspoken thought that they were no longer in control, and life had taken on a life of its own. When it came time to return to the dorm, she kissed him goodbye, and left him sitting on the stairs.

Saturday's date with the Justice of the Peace was not the last thing on Kate's mind as she turned out the light and burrowed under the covers. Luc's story of his short lived marriage in Alpine, and the inevitable turmoil that followed, intrigued her. She saw a man who allowed himself to be vulnerable, and at the same time venturing upon foolhardy, susceptible to the winds of chance, as he described it—a tumbleweed. There were no tumbleweeds in Missouri, as far as she remembered, making him all the more intriguing.

SEVEN

It was t-shirt and Levi cut-off weather for the first week of March and it was forecasted to get even warmer and dryer. Luc couldn't recall any rain since he landed in Sun City. He was not protesting; the predictability, the layback pace, complimented the solitary journey he seemed to be on. If he befriended a classmate it was confined to the subject they were studying, and that relationship never left campus. Big Bend State had been more like the community college he attended in East Texas, less demanding in quantity and quality compared to the rigors of his current course of studies. Without interruption, and social complications he was keeping up with the task. It was all work and no play; even shooting pool for beer and snacks took a back seat to his growing fondness for cooking Tex-Mex. He found out how easy and cheap it was to make tacos, chili, and burritos, and tortillas, hot sauce, and Monterrey Jack, became staples in his closet kitchen.

On the days he could get to the cafeteria Luc sat at the same table for every meal. It was situated near a block of windows where he could look out on to the common area. The cafeteria was a large unfiltered space where everybody's conversation mingled in a cloud of dissonance, and he chose one of the few semi-quiet spots where he could sit alone and read. Mark Twain was not on any of his class reading lists this term but once he got through Huckleberry and Tom, and into Twain's social philosophy he was hooked. He was absorbed in *Letters From the Earth* and didn't notice Kate as she put her drink on the table and sat down opposite him.

"Don't you look summery?"

Luc was wearing his daily warm weather uniform, and his Justin boots were replace by Jesus sandals. He was taking full advantage of living in a climate where snow was an anomaly, sunshine a given, and March waltzed in and out like lamb. He had not seen her since she nigh she had disappeared into dorm. Pleasantly surprised he put the book down.

"Seventy degrees today, it's the beginning of a heat wave."

"What are you reading that's so absorbing you don't notice when a gorgeous woman sits down next to you?"

"It's Mark Twain being totally irreverent toward conventional religion. Listen to this about pagans; 'They worship no god; and if we in goodness of heart do send a missionary to show them the way of life, they listen with respect to all he hath to say, and then they eat him. This doth tend to hinder the spread of light.' Don't you love it?"

"I sense a bit of irreverence coming from an ex-Catholic."

"Once a Catholic, always a Catholic is how the story goes. How's married life? You don't look any worse for wear, just as beautiful as ever."

It wasn't just flattery it was how he felt about the apparition that just sat down across the table.

"Well, we finally exchanged rings I can't wear; it was a two day honeymoon in the apartment with his roommate out of town, Albert's continuing with his Friday night fellowship, and it's still a sin to use birth control. How are you doing?"

"Okay I guess. I miss my friend, and it's only been a couple weeks. Are you still working at the registrar's? Stopped in a couple times to see if you were hiding behind the counter."

"I'm glad we're still friends after divulging our deepest secrets on God's doorstep. Anyway, I don't think he listens unless it's in a confessional. This is my last day. I've just come on campus today to say goodbye to everyone in the office. I didn't need the money, it was just a way to get out of the dorm. March is a pretty heavy month for me. Spring break during the second week is for UTEP students, not for Hotel Dieu. The following week is Mid-Terms, ending with Easter weekend. All the girls in the nursing school turn into God's mandatory handmaidens then."

"Mark Twain would say it's the ultimate male dominated celebration, the res-erection."

She didn't blink at the sarcasm. "I see why you like Samuel Clemens. Are you doing anything over the break?"

"I'm not planning on anything exciting, just downtime, working on papers, and studying for the upcoming exams. The GI Bill doesn't budget for exotic vacations. The cafeteria will open only on a limited basis so I'll be eating a lot of tacos. Do you and Albert have plans for the break?"

"Albert's off to the California coast with the boys. My schedule is lighter, but I still have courses and clinical sessions to attend. And of course the mandatory spreading of light, as Twain would say." She spoke with a touch of resentment in her voice.

"What a bummer. Albert's off to California, what's that all about?"

"It's not exactly California, they'll end up in Baja California down Mexico way. Another one of those March break pagan rituals." She played with the straw in her drink.

"Maybe not a bummer. Since we won't be seeing each other on campus anymore, are you still open for a Sunday visit after church? I don't think your neighbors will find it indiscrete, after all were both happily married."

"I haven't experienced the happily yet, you'll have to let me know when it happens. I'll check my calendar, but I'm pretty sure Sunday's are free for the rest of the semester. Is it a Missa lecta or Missa cantata mass you'll be attending?"

"Unfortunately it's the sung mass and as you know, it goes on forever. The nurses are part of the choir; you'll hear me before you see me. Now I have to get back to the office, they can't have a retirement party without me."

"Do you like enchiladas? I'm practicing my Mexican cooking skills."

"Becoming domestic are you. I like the green sauce."

She reached over and squeezed his hand, picked up her drink and walked quickly across the cafeteria. He followed her every step until she disappeared through the double doors. She reminded him of someone else he knew in East Texas whose Levis were so tight you could see her religion. He sighed and turned back to Mark Twain.

EIGHT

There were two reasons for Luc to attend Albert's Friday night fellowship, as Kate called it. One was to buy a bag of weed from Angel to ease the pain of going nowhere on vacation, and the other, out of curiosity, to see how the groom was handling marriage. He was half expecting to see Kate there, but she was noticeably absent. It was a far cry from his first visit; a couple standing by the kitchen counter, the Doors, *Strange Days* playing in the background, and through the sliding doors he could see bodies outside and inside the pool. He walked to the kitchen and grabbed a beer from the fridge acknowledging the couple hanging at the bar with a nod. Outside Albert was sitting on the edge of the pool talking to a woman in the water who was holding onto his legs; Steve was at a table with Angel along with someone he had never met. A couple other humans dotted the landscape. Considering it was a temperate evening it was not the wild and crazy party he was expecting.

"Well look who's surfaced. Excuse me Angelica, a ghost from the past just re-appeared. Stay in the pool you'll be safe from this guy."

Albert stood up and walked over to Luc. His track pants were wet from the knees down.

"I see you found the beer. Did you bring your bathing suit?"

"Hi Albert. I still can't wrap my head around jumping into water this early in the year unless it's at a health spa in a Jacuzzi. At any rate I recall you saying if I need a swim suit I'm at the wrong party, right."

"That's my Luc." They moved over to the table. "You remember Steve and Angel."

"Hard not to."

"And Danny here. You guys have something in common, both Nam vets. Pull up a chair. Someone roll up a doobie."

There was a plastic bag of marijuana and a packet of Zig Zag rolling papers on the table. Weed was so cheap and plentiful in El Paso there'd not be any room in the jails if they started arresting everyone, and the judges would have their dockets full, unable to prosecute real crimes. Unless someone was stupid and ignored protocol, marijuana use remained just below the surface, everywhere. Once it left El Paso, it was war on drugs and fair game for the DEA. Luc had a flashback from his time in Dallas where he learned to roll a number with one hand. His friend Billy Joe suffered through a bag of weed teaching him to go from a joint resembling a twist tie to one worthy of being passed around. Luc offered to do the honors, and picked up the zig zags. When he finished rolling a perfect joint with one hand Angel was impressed, and found a new customer, and a sale.

Other than the two ex-GIs, there was not much in common between guys at the table except they were in El Paso, Texas, attending university. Albert was an army brat whose number was high enough in the draft to escape service. Steve, with a little home town political pull escaped from Lubbock, Texas, and the draft, by attending UTEP. Danny Sauceda was as straight as the Texas Panhandle he grew up in, and along with half the high school football team, the Hereford Bulls, he joined the military upon graduation to hold off the yellow invasion. Danny it turned out was a real Nam vet, like Lenny his former roomate at Ozark Mountain College, who was knee deep in shit until he was medically discharged. The closest Luc got to the war was being stationed in Thailand where he could watch and listen to all the insanity around him. Danny carried with him a whole lot of combat baggage. He was one of the many silent wounded who returned from Nam without the words to describe the horror of war. He had been an army medic, saw the worst of it, and it broke the fragile thread keeping humans together as social creatures. He lived in his van. It was his safe zone. Angel, the only local native, avoided the draft, nobody knew how, and nobody cared.

Sports, politics, and the bar scene were the subjects of the evening. The topic of sex, whenever two or more males congregate, was like the back beat of hand-clapping and tambourines in gospel music. The primary topic, however, was not bikini clad Angelica in the pool, the first bullfight of the season in Juarez on Easter Sunday, or the fake news reports that troop morale was up and drug addiction among military personnel in Vietnam was down; it was the pending spring break gaucho invasion of the Baja.

"So far there's five of us ready to roll. Got room for one more if you're interested Luc."

"I don't know Albert. We've got mid-terms coming up at the end of the month. I don't even know where Baja is. What's the attraction?"

"Tell him Steve. This man's got his priorities all screwed up." Albert passed another number around.

"Baja is a Spanish word meaning beaches, booze, bongs, and bitches. Rosarita Beach in Mexico is an hours drive from San Diego. We leave here Saturday morning with the aid of a little crystal meth, to incite the brain's reward system, compliments of Señor Angel, and twelve hours later we're lying on the beach watching the sun go down over the Pacific. That's when the party begins, and doesn't end until we drag our sorry asses back here. Then, and only then do we worry about mid-terms."

The table went silent when Angelica climbed out of the pool, falling out of her bikini top while bending over to pick up her towel, straightened up, and glistened for the boys. They continued their lewd vigil until she closed the door of her friend's apartment.

"I think I'll pass. I'd like to score a lid of this stash we're smoking Angel. It'll be my vacation."

Luc brought them back down to earth; he was not into mental and physical self-degradation on a Mexican beach, nor could he afford it.

"*No hay problema amigo*. I'll be at La Cantina on Wednesday night. Check in with me there."

"What's La Cantina Wednesday night?"

Danny spoke up for the first time. He had been quiet taking in the conversation. Lay back and out of the limelight was his MO.

"It's a bar downtown, sells cheap beer. A popular place to hang out, for Mexicans and students. Where do you live Luc?"

"Stanton Street close to downtown, real close to the Cathedral."

"You're practically neighbors. Walk to the Plaza and you're there. On Wednesdays Steve and the literati of the Pass congregate to vocally discreate the world as we know it through poetry."

"I think Danny, you mean desecrate the world as we know it. We find in the profane the potential for truth." Steve prided himself on being a legal wordsmith.

"Discreate Mr. Steve, means to reduce your verbal aggrandizements to nothing. That works for me and what I generally hear." Danny sat back in his chair.

Steve was a Dylanesque poet. He could vehemently express contemporary social discourse; the Vietnam disaster first and foremost, but unlike Dylan, without anyone but the hardened activist giving a shit what he said. La Cantina was a place where you could rant and rave, and the consequence was a foregone conclusion—you'd wake up at home after a stoned poetry reading, not remembering how you got there, but thankful all the same.

"It's open mic Luc, so if you have a few poems to read I'll put you on the reading list." Steve was master of ceremonies, a position he carried for most things in his life.

"Maybe. I have a few poems I could share. Don't know if anybody would be interested in hearing them." We'll see."

Poetry was Luc's private catharsis, words stuffed in a drawer that revealed an inner self of how he viewed his reality. Albert's marriage never came up in the conversation. Angelica in the pool did, the broads in Baja did, but there was nothing said about Kate, which Luc found a little strange considering for all intents they were still on their honeymoon. Luc liked Danny, he was quiet but when he did speak up he added to the conversation. Danny told him he often parked his van outside La Cantina, it's his favorite spot to hang out.

Luc was confused, bordering on concern about Albert's relationship with Kate, but let it lie, and for the foreseeable future committed himself to hitting the books. He wasn't going to take the mid-terms lightly. He needed, for his own self-satisfaction, to score big on the grade point average that presently hovered below his expectations.

There were three weeks to make sure it happened and it looked like clear sailing. He'd start in with the books Monday morning. In the meantime, still rough around the edges after overindulging in beer and weed at Albert's get together, it was Saturday evening and he decided to wander over to the Rio Grande Bar. He thought he'd order some nachos and shoot a little pool. It turned into a marathon, holding the table most of the night, and the beers stacked up. He crawled home and fell into bed.

NINE

The Sunday morning church bells were a little more annoying than usual, and he buried his head under the pillow. The following choral and organ music lulled him back to sleep until the irritating doorbell forced him to sit up. He couldn't remember when someone last rang the bell or if he even had a doorbell. Jehovah Witnesses he thought as he put on his white linen housecoat compliments of Pam, and dragged his sorry ass down the stairs to the front door. Kate, all prim and proper, wearing a dress for the first time, was stopping by after church. He stood in the doorway silently staring at her, wondering if he was stuck in some lucid state between dreaming and waking.

"Good morning Luc," she said after an uncomfortable moment. "You could invite me in you know."

"Yes, right, hi Kate, come in. Come in."

He held the door open to let her pass, peering out the door as he closed it to see if anyone else was around.

"I'd almost given up on you," she said. "You must be a sound sleeper, and a late sleeper, it's past noon. I mentioned I'd drop by after church, you must have forgotten."

She stopped before climbing the stairs and looked him up and down.

"Am I interrupting anything?"

"No, not at all. With early morning classes I take advantage of sleeping in on the weekend."

It was an unlikely story but he couldn't think of what else to say. He hadn't forgotten, he just didn't believe it would happen. He ran his hands through his hair in an effort to comb it. She turned and bounced up the stairs. When she reached the top she stopped abruptly, and looked around the living room.

"What a cute place."

He stepped up behind her. "Can I offer you a coffee?"

"Not until you give me a tour."

Walking down the hallway she peaked into the kitchen, approvingly, the bathroom, noticing the little claw foot tub something she missed in her dorm, and upon reaching the bedroom, where the bed took up most of the room, she plopped belly down on the mattress, and peered out the open windows. She could make out Hotel Dieu to the rear of the church. He followed her from bus stop to bus stop and stood by the bed, his mind slowly beginning to focus on what was transpiring in front of him.

"Look, you can almost see my dorm room on the third floor. There's not much room between you and St. Patrick. Remember when it was a sin to miss mass? It may still be. Here you could almost attend mass and not get out of bed."

She rolled over and put her hand out for him to pull her up. They stood touching each other for an indecent moment.

"I'll have that coffee now."

He reluctantly moved aside and let her pass. The kitchen was U-shaped, a Formica table was attached to the back wall, with just enough room for two. Living in the dorm for four years Kate found his apartment cozy. Cute and cozy were not the adjectives Luc thought of. He was wide awake now and sitting across from her, he knew he looked like a bag of shit, but it didn't seem to bother her. They talked well into the afternoon about school, Missouri, East Texas, Ontario, the Catholic Church, past transgressions and future aspirations, and left the present hanging. The subject of her marriage to Albert was not broached, and best left to another time.

"Do you need to be anywhere soon?"

It dawned on him that maybe he needed get out of his housecoat and clean up his act. Having exhausted the coffee Luc's thoughts turned to sustenance.

"Back to the dorm by 5 if I want to catch Sunday dinner, otherwise the curfew on weekends for the coming weeks is 7 P.M. As a senior, with exams coming up, I'm expected to chaperone the lower grades in the study hall. I don't mind it's always a good refresher answering their questions."

"I've discovered this neat little bar just blocks from here. It's an authentic touch of Spain called Bar Español. Their food is great, and sometimes they have world famous flamenco dancers and guitarists. I've been there twice and ate paella, a Spanish rice dish, and another time it was their cochinillo asado. Its roast baby pig. Delicious. Would you be interested?"

"Sounds good to me, and I won't have to head back to the dorm for dinner, a double delight."

"I need to clean up my act and change before going out in public with you. Make yourself at home, I won't be long."

While he was in the bathroom she went into the bedroom, sat on the edge of the bed, and looked out the window at Hotel Dieu. *Too bad my rooms on the other side of the dorm*, she mused. She stood up, straightened up the sheets and fluffed the pillows. It was her nature. She sat back down with her back to the headboard, pulled her dress up to her knees, she hated how the nuns insisted they wear them down to the ankle, closed her eyes, and thought about where she was. Her escape from Missouri had not, until meeting Luc, provided what she hungered for. What she had read about in books she could never bring home from the library. Nursing was a means not an end, and experiencing a world beyond was her primary goal. Albert provided some of what she was after, but she knew it was not enough. She was impressed at first by his clever mind, a man with a mission on the road to success. He was her first lover, and she truly cared for him, but he was not Luc who'd been somewhere, explored life, challenged life, and was not taking life for granted. She began to understand this only after—immediately after tying the knot.

Luc came out of the bathroom, wrapped in a towel, and stood in the doorway to the bedroom. He expected her to be in the kitchen, or living room, and yet wouldn't want her to be anywhere else. He glanced out the window to see if the saints were watching. Kate rolled over on her elbow.

"Don't mind me, carry on. I've been studying anatomy for four years now, it's not often I get a chance to just enjoy it."

She watched him getting dressed. He was in great shape, and not the least bit shy. She was tempted to make a comparison, instead she put Albert completely out of her mind, for the moment. Luc thought a quaint Spanish bar on a Sunday afternoon, would be a quiet place to absorb a unique atmosphere, and continue their conversation. Kate's stories of life on the farm were captivating, as was her inquisitiveness when it came to Luc's trials and travels. She had the same fascination with anything other than what she grew up with, similar to most people he had met since coming to the South, and most recently Allison, isolated in Athens, Texas, tethered to the ranch. Kate was different, not so all consuming. As far as Luc could tell Kate was actively engaged in change.

Entering the dim, dusty Bar Española immediately on their right they passed half a horseshoe bench where an older gentleman buried under a sombrero cordobés sat engrossed in his guitar, playing flamenco. This was followed by a burnished bar running from the front of the room to the back with equal space on either side. On the pedestrian side wooden bar-height chairs from end to end, and enough room behind the chairs for anyone passing in and out to get cozy with those sitting down. Several indented benches were built along the wall that with attached table tops could accommodate two patrons each. Luc found one unoccupied bench near the end of the bar that was crowded, noisy, and smoky. Acting as if he knew what he was talking about, he recommended the Rioja red, a popular wine from northern Spain, and the seafood paella.

"Sounds perfect, I'm not much of a wine drinker, and I haven't a clue what paella is."

"To be honest, I didn't know what paella was until I ordered it last time, it has a few things in it you just don't want to know about. Tasty though, if you like seafood."

"I'm used to catfish and crawfish back home, but I'll try anything you recommend." She put the menu down, and added coyly. "Within reason that is."

He was discovering Kate had a tease about her, with a bent toward the sexual. She confessed her dining out and worldly tastes were limited to barbecues, church potlucks, and family trips to the Ho Toy Chinese restaurant in Columbus. As for wine, the only designated imbibers of wine in her life, until coming to El Paso, were her priests during communion, and Christ at the last supper. Her parents were staunch prohibitionists. The paella came quickly, hot and spicy, right out of a large cauldron in the kitchen, with crusty bread that was warm and sweet.

They ate without a lot of conversation, in part due to everyone else in the bar talking all at once, most speaking in Spanish, and listened to the flamenco music filtering through the crowd from the front of the room. They nursed the bottle of red wine, taking in the smoked filled stimulating atmosphere, while people watching. In the narrow confines of Bar Española, behind the bar the walls and counters were a patchwork quilt of pictures, paintings, plates, and wooden wine barrels, a clutterage of bullfight and flamenco memorabilia with only inches to spare between them. The patrons, in Kate's imagination, were all famous bullfighters, exotic flamenco dancers and singers straight from Spain. By six o'clock the crowds thinned out considerably, and they moved up to a space at the bar, closer to the music. The guitarist was playing Malagueña.

"This is one of my favorite songs. I first heard Malagueña when I was in the army in 1964, and living in the barracks. I was turned on to flamenco music when another GI who bunked down the hall was playing a recording of Manitas de Plata. Manitas who still today is considered one of the greatest living flamenco artist. I've been a fan ever since."

For Kate, country and western, and choir music had been the sum of her repertoire. Since she met Albert, rock and roll was added to the mix. Malagueña Salerosa however, could be heard anytime, anywhere in El Paso.

"I've heard the popular Mexican song called Malagueña Salerosa, you hear it everywhere."

"I learned the song has different interpretations Kate, Salerosa is about someone telling a woman from Spain how beautiful she is, and he knows because he's poor he'll never be her man." The variation he's playing is originally a Cuban song written for the piano, and Carlos Montoya, another famous flamenco guitarist, adapted it for the flamenco guitar."

"I'm impressed. And what's this one about."

"I'm not sure, maybe about a man telling a woman from Missouri how beautiful she is, and knows because she's married he'll never be her man."

When she turned to face the musician, he thought maybe he stepped across a line, until she turned back with a smile on her face, and laid her hand on his thigh.

They ended the day on the corner next to the Cathedral. Face to face they held hands, and she thanked him for a wonderful day. There was a goodnight kiss hanging in the air, and she left it there, squeezed his hands. He watched as she walked up the street and disappeared into the dorm. Luc felt like he had countless times before, standing on a platform while the train pulls away. Passing the steps to the cathedral on his way back to the apartment he could sense the Quasimodo staring at him from the bell tower, and there was an intimation of guilt. It should have been just an outing with his best friend's wife, but he wanted to think it went beyond a casual encounter, even if he was only fooling himself.

TEN

The street view of La Cantina was one large darkened window with a dirty glass doorway to the left of it. There was no signage on the window, and on the door painted on the glass three faded letters—BAR. Like the Bar Espanola the dim interior was long and narrow, bare light bulbs suspended on long cords from a high ceiling were hung haphazardly throughout the room, yellowed bullfight posters decorated the smoke stained concrete walls representing Manolete, El Cordobés, and others in various stages of sticking it to vicious looking bulls. At the far end of the cantina a small bar with four stools paralleled the left side, past that a lopsided banos sign hung over a small door on the back wall. The cantina, with the exception of replacing broken tables and chairs, and the advancements in indoor plumbing hadn't changed since it was opened in 1930.

To Luc's right, as he entered there was a low semi-circular platform beneath the front window, and on it a three legged wooden stool, and a Shure Super 55 microphone. He passed a couple engrossed in reading, sitting at a table near the platform. Luc thought it was not exactly an enthusiastic literary crowd waiting on the bard. It was 8 o'clock Wednesday evening when Luc settled on one of the bar stools and ordered a Dos Equis Amber. The bartender put the beer down in front of him, and stepped back. His face was a brown roadmap under a bald head with wisps of hair like a small ragged kippah. His native Mexican heritage prevalent in his high eyebrows and thin eyes. Under a wide proboscis a permanent smile propped up by prominent cheekbones. A bartender one could reveal secrets to.

"Is there a poetry reading here tonight?" Luc put a buck down, enough to cover his tab for the rest of the night.

"Sposed to be, I dunno. Kaitlin!" He yelled over to the couple. "Are you guys on tonight?" They waived confirmation and went back to reading. "All the action starts late around here. You're new here. You with the school?"

"Recently transferred from Big Bend State University in Alpine."

"Hey, I know the place well. It's where Albert went to school. You friends?"

"Sort of." His knowing Albert didn't surprise Luc.

"My name is Francisco Vázquez Reyes," he reached over the bar and shook Luc's hand. Luc estimated him to be in his fifties or older, yet his grip was that of a young man.

"I'm Luc. Luc Barbon. Glad to meet you."

"My family used to live in Boquillas, a village on the Mexican side of the Rio Grande, at the far end of Big Bend State Park."

"I know Boquillas, rode a donkey across the Rio Grande there. Drank tequila in the cantina. One light bulb in the whole village. Small world isn't it?"

Francisco lit up. He had fond memories of where his family came from. Boquillas being as far away from anywhere anyone could get to.

"You know, you and Albert are the only ones I meet who have ever been there." He put two shot glasses on the bar and filled them with tequila. Tequila Sauza, Luc's preference.

"On the house. Salud!"

People were slowly filtering in and filling the tables. Francisco was right on it having their drinks in front of them as soon as they sat down. He had a handle on everyone by name and their pleasure. Francisco's smile matched the sparkle in his eyes. Even in the dim light Luc could tell he belonged behind his bar moving about the space like it was second nature. As the patrons wandered in he was waiter, bartender, dishwasher, and Speedy Gonzales rolled into one. When he was able to take a break, he put another beer on the bar for Luc no questions asked. When Danny entered the cantina Francisco had a can of Tecate on the bar beside Luc who was watching Danny as he slowly made his way towards the bar, stopping at several tables to chat on his way. Luc turned to address the bartender.

"When did you move from the Big Bend country?" He was curious about Francisco's life in Boquillas.

"Too many years to count. I was niño when my padre moved here and opened this bar. He was candelilleros and made enough money for us to move to El Paso, and open this bar. There was a big demand in World War 1 for candelilla wax. It was used to waterproof tents and ammunition. It's illegal for Mexicans to smuggle wax across the border, but not illegal in the States to purchase it. Once it was a big industry along the Rio Grande, but not so much anymore." For a moment he was lost in recollection. "I graduated from the university when it was called the College of Mines and Metallurgy of the University of Texas."

"I was wondering if you'd show up." Danny pulled up the stool next to him nodding to Francisco a thanks for the Tecate. "Angel can't make it but gave me a lid for you.

Says it's on the house, welcoming a new customer. It's in the van, I'll give it to you later."

"I guess it's my day for on the house, Francisco just served me a shot of Sauza."

"Francisco will, on a dime, find a reason to share a shot of tequila. Isn't that right Francisco?" He raised his Tecate in salute. "His esposa doesn't want him drinking at the bar, so Francisco figures sharing good health with his customers is not what one would refer to as drinking, it was la empresa, business."

Luc noticed Danny was wearing the same well-worn sweat stained U.S. Navy Eagle P cap he wore at the pool.

"I thought you said you were in the army in Nam? You're wearing a navy cap."

"Yeh, I was an army grunt. I just like the looks of this one. Found it at an army navy store. I only take it off when I shower, and until I get plumbing in the van, that's hardly ever." The ability to find humor in one's circumstances was a quality characteristic of Danny.

He grabbed it by the duckbill peak, lifted it off his head and put it back on. Luc noticed he was bald, which fit into Luc's theory wearing a baseball cap causes men to lose their hair. It was the reason after leaving the Army he never wore a hat again, and why he still sported a full head of shoulder length hair.

"Did you bring something to read tonight?"

"Yeh, it'll be a first for me. I'm a closet poet. I thought I'd see what it's like to share. And you?"

"Last time I read a poem it was Dr. Seus." Danny looked towards the front door. "I see Steve has arrived. He'll get the show on the road, but only after we go out and smoke a number, compliments of the bag I brought you Luc."

Steve barged through the front door, stopping at every table on his way to a waiting bar stool. There was nothing quiet about Steve, and before he sat down he turned and introduced Luc to everyone in the room, making them aware there was a new poet in town to entertain with his wit and wisdom. Francisco placed a beer on the bar.

"You did bring some poems I hope. I have you third up on stage after me then Kaitlin."

He pointed to the couple Luc first saw when he entered the cantina.

"She's the Irish gem sitting with George. A senior in the Creative Writing, program. Her friend is a professor in the Art Department. Have you met them?"

"Sort of, from a distance."

"Great Poet, you'll love her. She just published her first chapbook of poetry, *When the Train Stops Moving*. We'll get rolling in a bit, let's go for a stroll first and smoke a number. Danny you buying?"

Out of deference to Francisco they didn't smoke inside La Cantina. His was probably the only bar in El Paso smoke free. Francisco's father had lung cancer, and smoked three packs a day before he died. It's why the walls were yellow.

Steve was on stage first thanking Francisco profusely for his ongoing hospitality, after which he launched into a poetic diatribe on the American game titled "Let's Destroy a Country." It was the inculpation of the American legacy of destroying countries through invasion under the banner of implanting democracy, destruction of the infrastructure, decimation of the existing lifestyle, corporate takeover of reconstruction, evacuation, and leaving them hanging for the next dictator. Steve rhymed off a litany of sins. The list of devastated military playgrounds was long, consummating in Vietnam. His second poem called "Operation Breakfast," was about Nixon's covert and illegal bombing of Cambodia, followed by a poem about the Mai Lai Massacre titled "Boys will be Boys," and ended with an ode to what Nixon called "an invitation to tragedy," inviting the National Guardsmen to kill the Kent State students "for hurling empty tear gas canisters" their way. Without a doubt Steve, was opinionated, and as obvious by the loud crowd response, in his element. Kaitlin McCrery, tiny and frail under a disheveled head of hair, looking perpetually on the edge of sobriety, followed Steve with a cutting harangue of Asarco, a smeltering giant with the second largest smokestack in the country, spewing toxic waste for decades into the lungs of El Paso and Juarez citizens. Barely reaching up to the microphone she spoke with a commanding voice.

The doobie along with a couple shots of tequila, compliments of his new found friends Danny, and Francisco, helped Luc get up the courage to read a couple poems. Unlike his predecessors on stage he avoided the insanity of the world around him, and focused on what he perceived as safe subjects. He wasn't out to save the world or wallow in doom and gloom. He spoke of his desert wanderings thinking the audience could relate to a desert slow time where the moisture hangs on sweaty palms of clouds, where the albino eye of the sun in a sky as blue as a postcard stalked the land with a hungry dog of a wind. He was pleased with the response he received, and afterward felt comfortable in his role as a new poet in the mix, if only for the moment.

Poetry was for Luc, one of the few ways he was able to express his inner feelings, and he never shared his passion with anyone other than his friend Pam in Alpine. So far she was the one person in his life he was comfortable enough with to share his innermost thoughts. He carried a portable typewriter around for years, and lost it in Arkansas. Pam gifted him with a 1964 Royal Safari portable typewriter in hopes he would continue writing. For Luc it was a means of recording thoughts and feelings, never to see the light of day. Until now that is. The invitation to a poetry reading stirred something in his subconscious never far from the surface, but occasionally needed a kick in the ass to arouse. Instead of heading for the Rio Grande Bar after class, in the days prior to the reading he had spent the afternoons and evenings at his desk, writing and revising. La Cantina and its eclectic patrons was right in his backyard, and had the makings of a home away from home.

ELEVEN

The days preceding spring break were a bust on campus inasmuch as the students were not focused on intellectual stimulation. The teaching staff were booked and waiting for a ride to the airport, and the administration and worker ants waited impatiently for the students to vacate the premise. March break was more reprieve than a break. Downtime was just that, sometimes a void in the scheme of things to fill with whatever made you feel good, or it was a vortex that sucked in all the empty spaces in your life. Downtime could be fatal if there was nothing there to occupy the emptiness.

Luc never had a problem being alone, this time, however, something seemed to subliminally aggravate the situation. With Albert out of the picture, off with the boys to the Baha, he thought, just maybe, he'd have some unencumbered quality time with Kate. She was married, however, just married, and there was no reason to believe she would or should be knocking on his door. What he did have though was a bag of killer weed to mellow his mind compliments of Angel. He did have enough course material to keep him busy day and night, and his typewriter was sitting silent on his desk waiting for him to explore with words the chatter in his brain. Downtime, however, has a way of tearing back the curtains and letting the darkness in.

Having stayed up most of Saturday night smoking dope and wallowing in rock and roll, his thoughts playing havoc with his mind. The Quasimodo church bells had zero effect on his sleeping in. He had left the door unlocked not counting on a visitor. It was while swimming in that stage of wakening, where the mind is in the borderland of self-awareness, neither asleep nor awake, he sensed an unexplained presence in the room. There was a hint of gardenia, or was it just a memory of Pam who loved gardenias. Kate was able to skip mass, and sat on the edge of the bed for some time before Luc began to stir. She thought the church bells summoning the faithful to service would wake him up, and she was prepared for her next move. Doing it though was a giant leap into what—she had no idea. She justified being there by having come to the conclusion Albert was a mistake; their marriage the result of rebelling against a stifling upbringing dominated by Carmelite nuns in breastless habits, and overbearing parents, who considered flesh to mean sinful tendencies. Luc was someone she could talk to, confide in, and when you're scared and afraid of the unknown, someone to hold on to. When he began to stir, she undressed, slipped under the sheet, and lay beside him.

It wasn't a dream, and it wasn't Cecilia, but it was saintly, Luc feeling he had died and gone to heaven. In the shadow of the Almighty two lost souls found a way to ease the pain of guilt by inheritance, satiating a hunger for love in the arms of soft and gentle. By late Sunday afternoon following a feast of flesh they had worked up a proverbial eat a horse appetite; bathed together to save water in the tiny claw foot tub, and headed for Pancho's, where they gormandized the all you can eat for a dollar Mexican Buffett. There was no study hall on Sunday, no need for Kate to return to the dorm any time before curfew. When they returned to the apartment they closed the bedroom windows on St. Anthony and St. Cecilia so as not be constrained by the Catholic guilt thing, and cuddled back under the sheets.

Kate was still locked into the evening study hall Monday through Friday but during the day she was on her own time with a list of excuses for not being around the dorm developed and fine-tuned over four years. The week that followed became vacation time, their spring break when they escaped the confines of the apartment, and explored on foot El Paso and Juarez with the freedom of anonymity. Returning to the dorm, attending the odd clinical were minor interruptions in what Kate considered honeymoon time with Luc, something she had not experienced with Albert. Juarez was a totally new and exhilarating environment, not a place young women went alone, and with Luc, holding hands and walking across the Paso Del Norte Bridge was, like the Bar Seville, stepping into a world she only imagined and longed for. The Kentucky Club with its 1930s décor, a probable but not conclusive birthplace of the margarita, and a history of literary and entertainment stars; Fred's Rainbow Bar, with sweetbread, avocado and ham sandwiches to die for, and the Mercado de Benito Juarez an open market, where the aromas assaulting the senses were magical moments that she had not experienced in the four years she had lived in the southwest. Mostly though, it was hanging out at the downtown San Jacinto Plaza watching the alligators that had been returned to the pond, walking the streets of old El Paso, and sharing time together as if this was the way it was, not the way it could be, if only. Luc fell in love with the moment, completely ignoring future ramifications, and any logistical facts accompanying such a fall. Kate, if she had a sense of what a fall from grace looked like, kept it to herself and played a game neither of them knew how to win. All things unravel over time if only to let you know tying the knot is like everything else in life, what can be done can be undone, and what is undone can be an invitation to learn how to tie a better knot.

On Saturday evening of the last weekend of spring break Kate managed, with the help of her roommate, to steal out of the dorm one more time. Albert and the boys would be returning Sunday. The following week she had a heavy school schedule heading into mid-terms. Their affaire de Coeur was coming to an end. It was after midnight, and exhausted, they fell asleep. Conditioned by the Sunday morning ritual of God summoning the faithful, Kate heard the call and woke up as the sun was searching for Quasimodo's bell tower, slipped out from under the covers, and stood naked beside the bed staring out the open double windows. She hadn't notice before, but it looked like St. Anthony and St. Cecilia were smiling. In spite of the sadness of having to leave Luc lying there with no idea when she would have a chance to return, she felt blessed for having share the time together. She knew she would not be seeing Luc for a while with exam week, followed by Easter week, when the nuns would be herding the student nurses through the Garden of Gemini, along the path of pain and guilt, toward the rapture of the resurrection. She dressed, and pausing in the bedroom doorway, wanting to kiss Luc goodbye, but knew if she did, she wouldn't be able to leave.

The bells were louder than usual. Luc could sense the empty presence beside him. He covered his face with the sheet, he could smell her sweat, and the memory of another morning waking to no one there caused him to jump out of bed, check the bathroom, the kitchen, and for no reason other than a helpless feeling of what the future might bring, stare out the bay windows. He knew she would have secreted into her dorm room early, and most likely be attending mass. He had a gut wrenching feeling this was the story of his life, and a premonition of things to come.

TWELVE

Angel promoted a onetime special for mid-termers; crystal meth was the poor man's cocaine. Danny convinced Luc it was guaranteed to increase his energy and alertness, supposedly improve intellect and problem solving, and help him stay up all night studying to boot. It was candy in Nam, and if he hadn't been wounded ending up with R&R on a hospital bed for six months he'd probably be hooked on it. Danny didn't give him the downside figuring it was just a short time fix for exam week, and he thought Luc was familiar with the drug. For Luc, after trying it for the first time, he found it worked, for a while. As Angel would say no hay problema. For Luc though the short term side effects were immediate; the screwed up sleep patterns, hyperthermia, and an accelerated heart rate making it difficult for him to focus in the exam room. Danny also left out the kicker, you have to increase the dose of speed to get the same effect, and if you're susceptible, which as it turned out Luc was, it could quickly grab you by the balls, and not let go.

By mid-week he was at La Cantina looking for Danny and more crystal. He didn't have a direct contact with Angel but Francisco could make the connections sooner than later. When Danny dropped by the apartment he could see Luc was a little wired, and advised him to take it slow and easy. Too much of the ice he told him would do just the opposite of what he needed it for, and melt his brain. Danny knew of what he spoke, and suspected that Luc was prone to addiction with this particular drug. Thursday morning's 7 A.M. exam was going okay until the reproduction processes of mitosis and meiosis, and the misogynist and misogamist stereotypes of the Wife of Bath got the best of Luc. He wrote off the test, and once back at the apartment he smoked a couple numbers to mellow out.

By the end of the week it was only a Good Friday because he was looking at one more exam in a course he was getting straight A's in. He was going to tackle it meth free. Lying back on his bed with the windows wide open, he was focused on the stained glass windows on the side of the church, particularly on St. Anthony, patron saint of lost souls, lost lovers, and straying partners, when the doorbell rang multiple times. Thinking it was Kate he flew down the stairs.

This was the first time Albert had ever darkened his doorstep. It was not the way Luc expected the day to start.

"What's up Albert? Good to see you." Luc struggled to say the words.

"We need to talk." His voice was devoid of energy, and without his sports coat, white shirt and tie he was totally out of character.

"Come on in."

Luc stepped aside to let him through, then looked around outside to see if someone else might be around before closing the door. Climbing the stairs Albert looked like he was dragging his dick behind him. Luc went into panic mode. He thought Albert had somehow found out about his involvement with Kate. He wouldn't hide it. He'd tell Albert the truth. He'd think of something. Albert fell on the couch and stared at Luc's desk, piled with papers and books.

"How's it going with the mid-terms?"

Luc cleared a space on top of the desk and sat on the edge. He wanted to take the high ground.

"I'm struggling. Last one this afternoon, thank God. You didn't come over to check on my academic progress. What's up? Can I get you a beer?"

"You got tequila?"

Luc went to the kitchen and returned with a full bottle of Sauza Blanco and two glasses, and set them down on the coffee table. Paranoia caused him to check to see if Albert was carrying a weapon before filling his glass and stepping back from the table. Tequila in the morning was not a good sign.

"It's Kate." He took a drink, and shook his head.

"It's not what you think it is." Was Luc's immediate response.

"Yeh it is. You've been drinking this blanco gasoline byproduct for as long as I've known you. You've got to join the John Wayne crowd and start drinking Sauza Conmemorativo Tequila Anejo."

"Can't afford it." Luc pressed on. "What about Kate?"

"I talked to her on the phone this morning. She's leaving me. Ending the marriage."

Fuck, he thought. There's probably a law in Texas you can shoot any bastard fucking with your wife. Luc picked up the bottle, filled his glass and leaned over the coffee table topping up Albert's.

"Did she explain why? What made her say it's over?" Luc was waiting for the hammer to fall.

"You got to help me understand this. We're just married for fuck sake!" There was anger in his voice this time. "I don't know what to do."

Luc took the high ground, and remained standing while Albert slumped on the sofa. He could move in any direction should Albert get violent. He tried again.

"Did Kate give a reason?"

"Her parents," He shook his head as if denying what he was about to say, "are arriving today and pulling her out of school. They want an annulment."

Luc, still holding the bottle of Sauza put it back down on the table. He didn't have to feign shock.

"Jeesuz Albert. How the fuck did this come down."

"Something about telling a priest in the confessional about our marriage, and it got back to the school. Dunno how in hell any of this shit happens. I don't even know what a goddamn confessional is."

Albert took a long drink and grimaced. He was searching for options and there were none. There was a cloud of silence in a room filled with questions and answers without solution.

"Anyway," Albert broke through the ice, "I came here because I needed to talk to someone about this, couldn't go to my school buddies, it would spread through campus like wildfire."

And your reputation would be shot, Luc suspected.

"Luc, you're the only Catholic friend I have, except for a few Mexicans. Thought you could shed some light on this shit. Know a way to fight it."

Luc pulled his desk chair up to the coffee table and sat down. He wasn't sure how, but thought he dodged a bullet, temporarily, and could give Albert advice on his no-win predicament.

"Confessionals are where you tell venial and mortal sins to a priest. Supposed to be private, between the confessor, that's Kate, and God."

"Sounds something similar to a lawyer's confidentiality. Right."

"You got it. At least in theory. The priest Kate confessed her supposed sins to, he is the conduit, and a conduit is not allowed to leak God's little secrets to the Sisters of Charity, or someone's parents, if that's what happened."

"What sin? What are we talking about here? How the fuck is getting married a venial or mortal sin?"

"To a non-Catholic who deflowered their daughter, that's most likely sinning against the honor your father and mother rule in the ten commandments. I don't know if it's a sin, maybe they think some Beelzebub seduced their innocent daughter or something, who knows what's in their mind. "

"Now you've lost me." He filled his glass. "So she confesses to this dude that she married me. What's supposed to happen after that? She's forgiven right?"

Luc was okay with where the conversation was going. It was as far away from what was running through his head, the thought of Kate being dragged off to Misery.

"Well, after guilt, confession and contrition comes the satisfaction of getting it off her chest. Kind of, I guess like confessing your guilt to a lawyer making the crime go away. Hold that thought."

He thought about that chest straining the buttons on her cowgirl shirt and knew he was losing it. He got up and scored a fat roach from the ashtray on his desk. Lit it, took a long deep inhale, and passed it to Albert.

"Once the guy in the box feels Kate is contrite enough he administers absolution. Absolution releases her of any guilt, or obligation. It has no effect on the parents or nuns outside of instilling rage."

"You got to be fucking kidding. Guilt or obligation for marrying me." Albert bogarted the roach.

"You got to remember, Kate's been brainwashed since she was baptized. On the annulment, that's like the pope's version of divorce, it ends the marriage as if nothing really happened and she's still a virgin like Cecilia in the stained glass window."

"I figured that one out. Maybe I need Steve to help me through this?"

"With the church for the right amount of donation a parent can have any marriage annulled.

"You're telling me they can just write me off, pretend I didn't exist?" He finished the roach and snubbed it in the ashtray. "And that means Kate's a virgin again for fuck's sake?"

Luc wanted to end the conversation. He didn't like the tone, and his focus switched from relief Albert had no clue about his elicit relationship, to a deepening concern for Kate.

"After two thousand years Albert, the Catholic church knows how to get around, and away with whatever they want."

"Is there anything you can think of? Anything we can do? They may already have dragged her off to the farm."

"I wish there was something we could do." And he meant it, but not for Albert. "Outside of trying to stop her parents from kidnapping her, if as you say she's still around, I can't think of a single move you could make. They've got you checkmated. The queen bee of the Sisters of Charity is a formidable barrier. Hotel Dieu is like the Vatican, a world onto its own, and the Cathedral is impenetrable."

"Jesus H. Christ!" He slammed his drink on the table.

"You got that right." Luc topped up both glasses. He just dodged a bullet, why did he feel a wound to the heart.

Albert left, without a solution to his pending loss, and what he also didn't know, the cuckolded husband had his revenge by crying on the rake's shoulder. Luc tackled the bottle of Sauza, smoked a couple numbers, and ended up for the rest of the morning on the edge of the bed looking over at Hotel Dieu, cursing St. Anthony and St. Celia.

THIRTEEN

Luc blew off his last exam on not so Good Friday and later that day hung out in a pew in the back of St. Patrick's church, hoping to catch a glimpse of Kate. Albert had come over to Luc's apartment right after Kate phoned him, and Luc didn't think they would have taken her away already; the parents, were devoted Catholics who wouldn't want to miss a good crucifixion. If anything they would be leaving sometime after Easter Sunday. It used to be the God living in the church outside his bedroom window was the one he went to when he needed someone to talk to, now the one person whose shoulder he wanted to lean against, was trapped within those Cathedral walls, and there was no entrance or exit for her. He knew foolhardy was one of the traits she liked about him. He also knew it was stupid sitting in the back of the church waiting for a miracle, but there was no other means to contact her, except maybe storming Hotel Dieu. The crystal he also snorted in the morning almost made that a viable option. There was a daily parade along the Stations of the Cross. Luc sat silently in the anonymity of the last row until people began to flock in to hear the Black Friday evening celebratory.

Returning to the apartment, he crashed and burned. He didn't hear the doorbell Saturday morning, and it wasn't until early afternoon he found the letter under the door at the foot of the stairs. Not having eaten since sometime Friday he was heading to Pancho's dollar buffet. He sat down on the front steps, afraid to open the letter thinking it might have been delivered by Kate, he feared she had knocked on the door and he didn't hear her. He slowly tore open the top and extracted two pieces of paper. One was from her roommate, noting Kate asked her to deliver her letter to him. The other:

Dearest Luc,

I will probably be on my way back to Missouri soon after you read this letter. Things haven't turned out well for me it seems. My parents and the Sisters of Charity gave me no option. I was told I would be kicked out of nursing school, and not graduate, nor would I get a recommendation if I wanted to continue elsewhere. Certification is my hard earned ticket to being able to eventually stand on my own. I thought Albert would be a way to start a new life and escape the confines of an environment where I am a second class citizen. He was something I aspired to be, self-assured, in control and capable of achieving whatever he wanted. I can't fault Albert for who he is, I can only fault me for not knowing who I am other than, as he said, the farmer's daughter. Our time together, from our little rendezvous on campus, dinner at Pepe's, exploring Juarez, walks through the streets of El Paso, and our intimate play under the nonjudgmental eyes of St. Anthony and St. Cecilia, will be something I can carry with me as a hallmark of what I expect out a relationship. You came along like a breath of fresh air and showed me there are possibilities, and that I could transcend the reality I was born into. The time we had together allowed me to know what I want is out there for the asking. I don't have to be other than who I want to be, and although I'm presently at the mercy of an unforgiving God, you've given me hope.

If you're ever in my home state of Misery, and need a nurse, look me up.

Love you—Kate

A wide concrete staircase led up to the entrance of St. Patrick's Cathedral. There were three gigantic ornate wooden doors most likely to accommodate individual entrances for Father, Son, and Holy Ghost. There were plenty of wimpled penguins, and sky pilots in long flowing habits milling around at the bottom of the stairs, while onlookers dressed to the nines in their Easter Sunday finest, crowded around like royal watchers waiting for the queen's coach. Luc, sat cross-legged at the top of the stairs on a brick sidewall waiting for the parade. He was wearing his finest Easter outfit: wrinkled tee-shirt, torn Levis, and Justins. On the inside he was coming down off a twenty four hour high, having depleted his supply of meth.

The illusion behind the Easter Parade which was now climbing the stairs in front of him was all about power, all about control of his soul, and Kate's soul. As the Knights of Columbus dressed in white, yellow, and purple feathers, silk capes, and shiny swords marched past him followed by pontifical vestments complete with miters and croziers—it was all too much of what kidnapped his childhood, and buried it in guilt and self-denial, and now, took the possibility of love away. They kicked him in the balls one last time with their power over Kate. Crumbling in a fit of laughter at the entrance to God's domain, he was free from them, but addicted to a new insidious power, more hands on than God.

FOURTEEN

The semester was ending soon, and finals were on the horizon. Danny was aware that Luc's class attendance was erratic, or nonexistent ever since he got his disappointing mid-term grades. In the weeks following Easter, Danny met up with Luc several times at La Cantina, where he'd been hanging out on a regular basis. He didn't know the whole story, but figured out Luc's funk might have some connection to Kate and Albert. On a Monday morning he tried Luc's front door. It was locked. After ringing the doorbell, and pounding on the door he contacted the landlady in the ground floor apartment who recognized Danny as a frequent visitor. She told him she hadn't heard any noise from upstairs for several days, and unlocked Luc's door for him to check on her border.

It took Danny a week to pull things together, straighten up the apartment, and his buddy. He had parked his van out front, brought in his mattress and parked himself in Luc's living room. Danny had immediately began the process of nursing Luc back to where he shook loose of the tremors, agitation and jaw-clenching side effects of the crystal meth. His training as a medic in Nam meant dealing with the battle wounded, and the drug wounded. Drugs, meth especially, were not a panacea for what kept Luc from dealing with his underlying issues. On the contrary they only exasperated the situation, finally getting the best of him. He had bypassed Danny, his normal conduit for street drugs, and had gone straight to Angel for the crystal. Angel assumed Luc had it under control, not realizing it was the other way around. Depressed over the Easter turn of events, and his shredded GPA, the ice had grabbed his addictive personality by the short and curlies and chased him down the rabbit hole. Drugs had always been a pleasure not a problem. This time there was a monkey on Luc's back.

Benzo and weed was what Angel recommended to help bring Luc down. Having been through it all himself, Danny had taken a different route to sobriety. He had an escape plan for his buddy, time tested on himself. Luc needed to avoid any temptation that might trigger a relapse; no drugs, eating well, and focusing on the positive. If he had known about Luc's history with Jack LaLanne, alias Pissant, while working as a trainer in Dallas at the Ambassador Health Club, he would have had him doing pushups non-stop. That would be another story for another time. It was labor intensive but Danny managed to helped Luc pull himself together enough to start taking care of business even to the point of having an occasional Lone Star, under the guise that it was labeled the national beer of Texas. Venturing out meant rest and recuperation at La Cantina.

"What now?"

Danny put the big question on the bar as they nursed a brew. Another military medic treatment. It was Sunday and La Cantina was empty. Hector was filling in for his dad Francisco, who after thirty-five years of marriage decided to take his esposa on a honeymoon to Mexico City. It was the first break from behind the bar since he graduated from UTEP. Hector was also following in his dad's footstep as a university student.

"Well, my semester's TARFU; totally and royally fucked up. There's no use trying to salvage the finals. I'll withdraw before the deadline next week and hope for the best. An incomplete, if I can get it will at least keep me in the game. I could find a job here; work till I get my shit together, and tackle university again in the fall. Trouble is my resume is a tabula rasa. Maybe I could try bartending. Hector here is taking courses and working nights. He probably could use some help."

"Bartending here will not put you on the road to salvation Luc, or make you rich. On the contrary, look at Hector, he's a broke and lost soul. Right Hector?"

Hector flipped him the finger. "Right Pachuco."

Danny Boudreaux was joking, yet serious, knowing breaking the habit was like walking on thin ice. Luc would need support to keep his head above water. Danny knew of what he spoke. Like Luc, he escaped out of the hole he was born in by joining the US Army, only in his case, to end up in a foxhole. Luc also felt a friendship with Danny considering male bonding for him had been few, and somewhat precarious. As a math equation, two minuses here made a plus. *What Now* rattled in Luc's brain like a pinball trying to stay out of the hole. He had two months to kill before the fall semester, enough money to live on tacos for the duration, a library to occupy his mind, and a friend to hang out with to keep him on the straight and narrow. Danny taking a couple summer course, was not an option for Luc.

"I guess I'm not ready to tackle any courses at this juncture. Would have like to explore the Drama Department to see what I could get involved in. I played a part in the school play at Ozark Mountain College, in the role of Thomas Diafoirus in Molière's *Blythe Spirit*. That was at Big Bend State, not exactly a repertoire, but I'm looking forward to another kick at the can someday."

With no sign of customers Hector had pulled up a stool behind the bar and half listened to the conversation. He jumped in with a suggestion of Luc getting involved in the El Paso Community Theater.

"There calling for males to try out for a play by Rob Urbinati called *Death by Design,* for their summer production. "

"How do you know that Hector?"

"Like you Luc I'm interested in theater. Not acting, I help with the lighting. It fits with my UTEP courses with the School of Engineering."

"There you go Luc, that'll keep your mind occupied day and night. Just maybe keep you out of trouble. Plus give you a step up when you're ready to return to the academic grind." Danny thought Hector's suggestion was a good idea.

Given a name and address, Luc followed up on Hector and met with David Primlott the director of the Theater's upcoming summer production. After a cold read from the script and a rundown of Luc's interest in theater, David convinced him to take a small part as Jack, the Cockney, charming, clever chauffeur in his twenties, Rob Urbinati's *Death by Design.* It was a comedy with a murderous bent, replicating the wit of Noel Coward, and the whodunit of Agatha Christie, as a motley assortment of guests descend upon the country home of a married playwright and actress. Set in an English country manor in 1932 David had a difficult time finding cast in a community where eighty percent of the college population was Hispanic. Not an easy recruitment for an English comedy. The play was a hit, and Luc was hooked again on theater. He had no plans, however, to move to Hollywood. Another of Nurse Danny's recommendations was make new friends in recovery, the theater crowd fit the bill. In the process he discovered David was gay and was introduced to the gay scene in El Paso. Luc figured it was a pre-requisite for directing plays. It was different from what he had been previously exposed to in that David's world was out of the closet, open, cosmopolitan, and in your face. The play itself was fine for a laugh, but the real fun was backstage and hanging around cast and crew. Even more so when at the end of show party he was introduced to two temptations, one under control with a watchful Danny in attendance, nursing a beer for the night, and one in the name of Colette Boudreau. Turns out she just happened to have the same blood running through her seductive body as the Francophone who, when it came to one specific addiction had no control, and Danny had no remedy for love potion number 9.

Colette was a born and bred product of les Acadiens, Louisiana Creole with roots going back to the Canadian-American territories in the 17th century. She was a descendent of a mixed-race class of women who were educated and had property. They made up the wealthy and influential artisan class. Her father, a virulent Captain in the army stationed at Fort Bliss was on a tour of duty in Vietnam with a 50/50 chance of coming home in one piece, if at all. Colette, a graduate of UTEP in Liberal Arts, worked at a men's store catering to David and his gay friends, all of whom were over the top fashion conscious, some even chichi. Like Jacques Guillaume Lucien Amans' classical portrait of a Creole woman in a red tignon she had light tan skin and an air of coquettish sensuality, and an aura of intrigue and speculation about her. To Luc that made her instantly standout as someone of interest. Once he mentioned his French background; furriers landing in Quebec in the 1500s, his mother's side of the family being Francophone, he also ended up very high on her interest scale. On their first encounter they talked into the wee hours of the morning sitting out on the porch on David's teak swing bench while the gaiety inside his apartment roared on with Babs, Deva Diana, and Bathhouse Bette. Colette's family were from New Orleans. She had a French-Catholic background, analogous to Luc's. For some reason, Luc couldn't get away from the Catholic connection.

Turns out Colette lived in base housing with her mother, and hated it. With her father overseas her mother was having an affair with a sergeant first class Colette thought low class. The men's store she worked at called Gin &Tonic was located downtown, and a short distance from Hôtel Rouge. It didn't take long for her to start dropping by after work, and Luc the gentleman he was, didn't find it necessary to analyze their relationship. She was 21 and physically active, he was more than capable of accommodating her needs without commitment. What could possibly go wrong with that arrangement? She became aware of the circumstances of his 'marriage' and the tumbleweed tendencies guiding his life. She also knew he was still focused on obtaining a degree. No matter at the time, likeability turned to lust, and although they didn't have much in common besides food, sex, music, and more sex, it worked for them. Colette loved to cook and Luc loved to eat: gumbo, chicken creole, jambalaya were second only to his cooking talents for Tex-Mex.

Danny moved back to his van when the inevitable transpired. Luc was aware of the conflict Colette had at home, and when the tension boiled over and she sought refuge, Hôtel Rouge had a room available underneath the watchful eyes of St. Tony, St. Cecilia and her cherubs. When Danny told Luc Hector's father was back at La Cantina, his retirement short lived due to his esposa never ending complaints about him always being underfoot, it was time to celebrate Colette moving in. When Luc introduced Francisco at La Cantina to Colette it was an event that brought out the tequila. Luc allowed himself one shot of Sauza and a Lone Star, it was getting close to re-enrollment at UTEP, and the farmer's daughter interlude had sadly gone fallow.

FIFTEEN

After his disastrous first semester, Luc needed faculty support in re-registering. On probation he required a sponsor from the English Department to vouch for him. Professor Irving came to the rescue. Director of the Drama Department, he noted Luc's previous experience and as limited as it was Luc at least came with some positive credentials. Irving required an "older" student to play a part in the fall production of *Who's Afraid of Virginia Wolf*. Unfortunately the present stock of eligible students suitable for the role was tenuous at best. Luc fit the bill and was recruited for the part of George, the male lead in the play. Professor Irving's influence managed to get him enrolled without a hassle. The fall semester with a full load of classes, and what certainly would be a grand theatrical challenge subsequently kept Luc spinning day and evening. He stayed away from the temptation of drugs even as Colette and Danny carried on. Mind altering anything didn't work well with memorizing George's role. Scotch on the other hand went along with the play's alcoholic couple in 'Whose Afraid' and Professor Irving, who also liked his scotch, made it almost mandatory after every rehearsal to indulge in a nightcap or two.

Needless to say by the end of the semester, although successful from a grade point average, and his revived standing in the English Department after a surprising crowd pleasing performance, Luc's romance with Colette had taken a back seat. It required resuscitation, if only from his perspective. On her part Colette had no intention of sitting around and waiting for attention, she was thoroughly enjoying the best of both worlds, playing at marriage while living the single life. The end of the school semester and the Holiday Season Luc surmised was the perfect time to pull it together on the home front. Angel came to the rescue with some jolly green and snow. Danny donated the New Mexico State tree, a live pinon Christmas tree. Luc and Colette spent a romantic few days breaking in a pillow-top bed at Josefina's B&B in Las Cruces. They were back, for the moment, to when they first got together. By the time they came up for air it was a new year, and Luc was presented with new problems.

The ice melted in the Gin & Tonic, the store closed due to the owner's demise. Colette was out of a job, and not in a hurry to find another. Luc was now paying rent at the apartment, Pam's parting gift of a year's rent had dried up, and when the eagle shit it was for an unmarried vet and barely covered registration and books. The holiday extravaganza took the bank account to a new low. Luc needed a job, in order to maintain his living arrangement with Colette, one which didn't conflict with his classes. Theater would be history, much to Professor Irving's disappointment, for *Who's Afraid of Virginia Wolf* had been a feather in his director's hat. His spring production *Waiting for Godot*, by Samuel Beckett, which he selected for his budding student actor would have to wait for another semester. To Luc it seemed to be a pattern. By the time March came in like a beggar looking for loose change the honeymoon was becoming a waning moon, Job hunting with a full schedule of classes presented its own complications, while evening and weekend positions were equally limited. His relationship was strained, to put it mildly, not from Luc's perspective, he was too preoccupied trying to figure things out; it was Colette's having to curb her spending habits that did not go over well.

Luc was looking at dropping a couple courses, allowing him to expand his job search, until one day stumbling across KTEB 1500 A.M. There was no help wanted ad, no indication it was in the market for a radio announcer, and Luc's meager employment track record had nothing to do with any prerequisites for working in a radio station. He dropped in to the impressive windowless stone façade building simply out of curiosity about what it would be like working as a disc jockey. The station manager and on air weatherman Berke Montana, leaned back on the front edge of his desk, and was quite animated as he rattled on, talking a mile a minute. A graduate of Ball State University, he told Luc how impressed he was by a fellow alumni David Letterman, an anchor and weatherman on an Indianapolis television station WLWI and Berke had followed in his footsteps. After two years as an army Radio and TV Broadcasting Apprentice stationed at Fort Bliss, upon discharge he was scooped up by KTEB television. Before Luc even knew if there was a job opening and for what qualifications, Berke rattled off his, and the stations complete history in the broadcasting world. Berke then had him sit down in front of a mic and read the news. He was taped, and told the station would be in touch. Fortunately Colette had had a telephone installed in the apartment, something she insisted she couldn't live without. Luc wrote the interview off as a weird but informative interview, until he got a phone call early the next morning, the first one he had ever received. Berke told him if he was still interested in working for them, the owner of KTEB would like to see him at 11 o'clock. He was advised not to be late. Berke had liked what he heard on the tape and passed it on to his boss.

They were interested in Luc's voice, not so much the package it came in.

His Canadian accent and military service landed him the interview with Mr. Eulice Fontaine Smoot who was the founder of the biggest radio and T.V. station in El Paso, and one-hundred percent military. Not having been asked to take a seat Luc stood at attention in front of an enormous mahogany desk, while Mr. Smoot reviewed his résumé. Luc took the moment to scan the wall behind him. A Confederate flag dwarfed the Stars and the Stripes below it. On either side of the red flag with the blue saltire cross were framed memberships in the Sons of Confederate Veterans, and the American Legion. Luc was well aware El Paso was a military town but couldn't make the connection to the rebel flag.

"Luc Bourbon, what kind of a name is Bourbon?" His tiny voice didn't match the bulky figure filling to the point of overflowing the high-back leather chair.

"It's Bar-bon sir, French Canadian." Luc was used to the mispronunciation having been here before a few times.

"Three years Army Signal Corp I see. What did you do there? Did you serve in Vietnam? Did you see combat?"

"My job was to search for the enemy. They were going to send me to Nam, but needed me in Thailand to guard the rear, and eventually after returning to the States patrol along the Mexican border looking for protruders.'

"A missed opportunity to share in the glory of battle."

Not looking up he continued perusing the résumé, while Luc focused on a framed daguerreotype of a confederate officer, on Mr. Smoot's desk, a stalwart fellow in military uniform, a mop of hair and mutton chops draped his stern face, and his arms were folded, as if to indicate he had not lost upper body parts in battle. Luc knew from his experience applying for work at the Ambassador Health

Club in Dallas, turning the interview around by inquisitive comments on the identifiable passion of the interviewer somehow helped the hiring process. In this case it was the striking resemblance the soldier in the framed daguerreotype had with Mr. Smoot.

"If you don't mind me asking sir, Luc pointed to the picture, is he a relative? There's a resemblance."

It worked momentarily. The stern face softened, and he put the résumé aside.

"Major General Carter L. Fontaine." Mr. Smoot reached over and turned the photo toward him. "Fought in the Mexican-American War, resigned the Union, and fought under the confederate flag. End of the war, at the invitation of Maximillian, Confederates were invited to resettle throughout Mexico. Major General Fontaine came to Northern Chihuahua."

"What happened to him?"

"After Maximillian was killed by a firing squad in 1867, the Confederates left Mexico, and those who didn't were killed by bandits. My great, great grandfather escaped north to what eventually became El Paso."

"Are you related to those pictures behind you? I recognize Robert E. Lee." Stupid question but Luc seemed to have hit a nerve.

Lined up on a large oak leather top cadenza were half a dozen daguerreotypes of Confederate soldiers, and lying in front of them a staff and field officer's saber. Mr. Smoot swung his leather chair around and pointed at each one, naming them as if they were family members.

"They're all heroes and they all learned the art of war in the Mexican-American conflict. It was their war college and preparation for fighting the Civil War. He pointed to each: "Old Pete" Longstreet, wounded in Mexico, "Blizzards" Loring lost an arm there, Puss-in-Boots" Maury, wounded. Maury went on to found the Southern Historical Society in 1868. I'm sure you recognize "Old Jack' Stonewall Jackson, and yes the great one General Lee. Few people know about the Confederates in the Mexican War."

He swiveled back to face Luc and changed the topic. "What do you know about baseball?"

Luc knew as much about baseball as he did about the Confederate Army—Jack Diddly.

"Not a whole lot sir. I know it's a great American sport. Growing dup it was all hockey."

"Well son, by the end of this season you're going to be an expert. You'll be bringing in over the airwaves, to the fine people of El Paso, all the Texas Rangers games. This will be their first season playing in Texas, and you'll be with them all the way to the World Series. My man Berke will set you up. The season starts April 7, and I expect you to be up at bat and ready for a home run."

He stood up, leaned over the desk, gave Luc a limp handshake, and sat back down. The interview was over. He was hired, although unsure of what the job required, and how baseball fit into it.

Luc couldn't help but comparing the interview to that of applying for the physical trainer job in Dallas. The man who hired him James P. Dexter, Executive Director the Health Club ignored the holes in his resume, got his name wrong, and hired him on the spot without describing what for. Before Luc closed the office door Mr. Smoot gave him one last direction.

"One more item Mr. Bourbon, dress code here is shirt, tie, and sport coat at all times."

SIXTEEN

Luc was confused about the dress code considering the deejays booth Berke showed him was in the basement, and his shift would be nights, starting after everyone in the building went home. Berke's job description for Luc was straight forward; pull in the nightly baseball games, plug in the commercials and news, and if you need to fill in air time for rain delays, play like a disc jockey and throw on some music, just never let a second go by without sound. He gave Luc some reading material on the history of the station and told him he'd fill in all the paperwork, and show him the ropes starting Monday morning. Berke had been temporarily covering the evening shift since the previous DJ eloped at the end of March with Smoot's daughter. His now son-in-law, a graduating senior in media studies at UTEP, didn't want to continue nights now he was married. He still worked for 'Daddy' though, covering the weekend shifts.

Goodwill Industries was Luc's first stop after leaving the KTEB studio with job in hand. He needed a white shirt and tie, and a sport coat. He had not owned a tie since his discharge from the Army in 1967. Next stop was home to give Colette the good news. At least on the surface of it all, he thought was good news. For one he didn't have a handle on what the job really entailed, how it could affect his home life with classes starting early in the morning, and working until the last inning or the end of a double header. Colette was thrilled, six hundred a week would go a long ways toward keeping her happy.

There was not much room for hand holding in the sound proof studio the size of a walk in closet, hidden in the bowels of the building. Berke demonstrated how to talk into the mic, and control the environment without getting off the swivel chair. He ran through every flip switch on the board. Flipping switches brought in the national news, weather, and sports, and the station's primary purpose for hiring someone who didn't know what the inside of a radio station looked like—pulling in the Texas Ranger's nightly play-by-play. Berke personally prepared the minute by minute nightly schedule that would be waiting in Luc's mailbox when he arrived in the evenings. The cassettes with the commercials, community service bulletins, and announcements were stacked in a cassette holder in order of appearance. When he reached the cassette with the national anthem he was through for the shift. There was little room for innovation. Technically he was sitting in a cockpit on automatic pilot. Timing was the name of the game. Above a glass wall overlooking a conference room below, where community interviews were conducted, the clock, the size of an aluminum wash bucket was strategically lined up with the microphone. His shift was measured in seconds; the big hand counting down from the time he flipped a switch pulling in the 6 o'clock news from NBC, until he plugged in the final cassette following the 11P.M. news (again not counting for rain delays, and double headers).

On the rare day off for the team, usually on a Friday or Monday, Luc was expected to play music. Berke had him practicing over and over again cueing the two turntables on either side of the desk keeping in sync with his voice and the second hand. Once Luc mastered it he now felt like he was in a cockpit flying a 727. There was a large selection of vinyl on the wall behind him. A God fearing station, Mr. Smoot did not tolerate rock and roll. His choice of music was laid out for him: Big Band, swing jazz, and movie musicals. He was okay with the choices, it was what he grew up with at home. Sitting alone in a soundproof room, watching the long hand on the clock jerk around, the little hand tripping on the minutes, listening to the drone of sports announcers, didn't add up to Luc's perception of a radio disc jockey, but what did he know?

With Luc's time was wrapped up in studies and work from morning to midnight, downtime was carved out for sleeping, and Colette didn't seem the worse for wear. The bank account was fat city, and she talked him into finally leaving Hôtel Rouge and moving into an Upper Valley townhouse in a suburban complex bordering New Mexico and the Sunland Park Race Track. Once her domain was furnished, mostly from garage sales, and it began getting too hot to lie around the community pool, to fight off the ensuing boredom she adopted two male café-au-lait miniature French poodles. She named them BamBam and Bubba. Weeknights without a car Danny became her playmate. He came with a constant supply of weed, and hanging out with him at her now favorite neighborhood bar except for Saturday and Sunday, became a nightly affair.

In 1959 Doniphan drive was the main highway through El Paso. One day a country singer Marty Robins heading to Dallas, stopped in at a bar along the way for refreshments, and upon continuing his trip wrote a song that made him a superstar and Rosa's Cantina famous. The line in the song, "Night time would find me at Rosa's Cantina," worked for Colette, with the bar close enough to the townhouse to where it became her home away from home, even when Danny was not around. She managed to pick up some part time waitressing on weekends. Contributing to the household finances was her reasoning which included feeding and manicuring her dogs. She felt right at home in a west Texas watering hole for local cowboys and bikers.

Luc's quality time with Colette came on weekends, and took a big hit. He felt like a third wheel on a hog hanging out with Danny at Rosas Cantina drinking beer all night while Colette worked the tables, and the patrons.

In spite of the long hours, limited home life, due to daytime classes, and more baseball than Luc imagined for a lifetime, it all worked out until right after he enrolled in a couple summer courses. Berke informed him Mr. Smoot liked what he was doing and wanted him to take over the Sunday morning shift through September. It turned out his son-in-law needed a break from his media studies at UTEP, and was planning a tour of the confederate states with his bride to visit relatives and to soak up a little confederate history. Berke explained the shift would expand Luc's broadcasting knowledge, and add a few more bucks to his paycheck. Neither of which turned Luc's crank, but he understood the assignment was not debatable. The Sunday morning shift was an eye opener at 7 A.M. and dragged along until noon. Luc's job involved opening not closing with the national anthem, sitting back and plugging in commercials, and news breaks following each evangelical half hour radio tirade about the devil's hold on humanity. Since Luc didn't have a TV, or listen to A.M. radio, it was a new experience, and it convinced him a career as a disc jockey might not be in the cards. The only saving grace being, with everyone at church, he started smoking a doobie before hitting the airwaves.

In spite of the extra shift, summer gave Luc some breathing space both at home and at school. He took only two make-up courses for the ones he previously blew off as incompletes, giving him some daylight to spend with Colette, and the dogs. He even picked up a second hand TV to watch the news. At work bringing in the news between fifty minutes of mind-numbing baseball—the Texas Rangers were on their way to losing around a hundred games, perked Luc's interest in what was happening in the real world. The weather report seldom varied, however, the quagmire in Nam was still a hot topic, Watergate was beginning to heat up, and George Carlin was arrested for public linguistic obscenity. Colette loved Mexican soap operas. She also spent more time waitressing at Rosa's Cantina without Danny who was more involved with his summer courses.

Mid-August Luc got his summer grades—straight A's. He registered early for the fall semester, paid his fees, and it was time to celebrate entering the last steps on the ladder toward his degree along with Danny. Colette insisted they party at Rosa's Cantina starting Saturday afternoon. By early evening Luc knew he wasn't going to make the Sunday shift and called the station to inform them he'd come down with a case of food poisoning from salsa left out in the heat too long. It was the first day he had taken off since starting the job. Mr. Smoot was not happy.

SEVENTEEN

Classes for Luc began the last week of August. It was on the Friday before the holiday weekend when Luc was informed that starting after baseball season the station was switching to a Christian format. Berke explained. Mr. Smoot was a Sabbatarian, and follower of Herbert W. Armstrong's Worldwide Church of God. KTEB was going to a weekly schedule of transmitting a mixture of Christian music and Christian talk and teaching, which included Garner Ted Armstrong's *The World Tomorrow*, *The Happy Goodmans*, and *Thurlow Spurr and the Spurlows* among a flock of preachers. For some reason Berke was excited. The kicker was Mr. Smoots son-in-law, back from his journey down confederate memory lane, was now taking a couple post graduate courses, and would be taking over the weeknight shift, and Sunday would be Luc's last day. Two weeks' notice would have been nice, but then again this was Texas. He should have told Berke to shove Sunday, but he knew he had a feeling he would be needing the money.

When Danny brought Colette home after her shift at Rosa's Cantina, her normal response to the sad news would have been to add a few choice maledictions to the lexicon of the American Heritage Dictionary. In spite of the ramifications of Luc's zero chances of finding another evening job paying anywhere near what he was pulling in at radio station, with the prospect of having to move, and no longer able to take BamBam and Bubba for their weekly manicures—Colette took it rather lightly. Luc figured it was a sign things would work out. Danny produced a couple joints, and they decided to worry about it after the Labor Day weekend. Colette was not scheduled to work over the holiday but Saturday afternoon she told Luc they needed her to cover for another waitress in the evening. Instead of hanging out at Rosa's he had Danny drop her off at work and they proceeded on to La Cantina.

"*No hay mal que por bien no venga*, nothing bad comes without some good." Francisco poured the three amigos, and himself a full shot of tequila.

"Sometimes it's hard to find that good Francisco. I guess I thought being a disc jockey I was on my way to the good life."

"Do you want the good life Luc, or the life that's good for you."

Every good bartender it seemed had a little spiritual advice in them. Danny raised his glass.

"I toast what's good for you Luc. If you ever figure it out let us know the secret. Salud!"

When Luc arrived home around midnight Colette was already asleep. Normally she stayed at Rosa's until it closed to help sweep the bodies out the door. Without waking her or the sleeping beside her, Sunday morning a reluctant DJ sat in front of the mic waiting for the national anthem to come to its inevitable conclusion. Mr. Smoot recommended he stand with his hand on his heart when it was played, a move he ignored. Berke had left Luc's final paycheck on the bulletin board. The morning gave him plenty of time to contemplate the new reality. Getting married to increase his GI Bill was out of the question, been there, done that. They would have to scale down, that was evident. Colette would have to curb her spending, and earning a few bucks waitressing under the table would help. Maybe he'd look into bartending nights, there were plenty of bars in El Paso. It had nothing to do with the hallelujah music emanating over the airwaves, but he was optimistic. And on the up side, he'd have an opportunity while job hunting to spend more evenings with Colette. As Francisco said, he needed to find the good in his present predicament. When he arrived back at the townhouse after his shift, Colette was nowhere to be found. BamBam and Bubba were hyperactive. He found a note on the fridge door.

Animal just got a new hawg, and we're riding to catch the Doobie Brothers in concert Monday at the Roosevelt Stadium, in Jersey City. He says with a tailwind we'll just make it. Won't be back. Feed the dogs.
P.S. took the dope, sorry.

Until Danny pulled up in front of the townhouse, Luc was able to gather up enough roaches to fend off the need for something stronger, much stronger than marijuana. Luc had called La Cantina on the half chance Francisco could get in touch with him. He lucked out, La Cantina was open all Holiday weekend, and Danny was parked in front. He had read him the note, it was all he needed to say, and Danny was on his way with a bottle of tequila, donated by Francisco, and the devil weed he saved for the holiday weekend, for what he now knew would now be a long Laborious Day. Prohibition was no longer a concern for Nurse Danny, his patient seemed to have his life under control, a least up until the present crisis.

"Why didn't I see this coming Danny? We've been together for almost, what a year, you'd think I'd recognize something was wrong with the relationship. Losing Colette, and the job in one day makes me think there's another strike coming across the plate."

"Keeping with your baseball analogy, I don't think you ever see these things coming until the games over and you get to review the reruns."

Luc leaned back on the couch with his hands holding his head.

"I don't know how baseball got into the fucking conversation. I think I've been brainwashed. The Texas Rangers were a losing team, I can relate."

He was searching his mind for some clue to explain his present mess.

"You were with her at Rosa's Danny, did you have any clue about this? Did you know the guy?"

"Animal. Yeh, from a distance. He was one of the biker regulars. They had something in common. I thought it was just flirtation, and didn't think it was my place to elaborate on it. To me it was just Colette being Colette."

"It's what attracted me to her when I first met her. She was just fun to be with. We could talk about everything...she was a talker, with a sensual Louisiana French accent, and heady way of teasing the conversation. She loved to tease..."

Luc poured himself another glass of tequila. Danny lit up a doobie and passed it to him. Spending time at Rosa's over the months while she worked there, Danny caught the connection with the bikers and figured something was happening while Luc worked the air waves. At first his role was keeping Colette company, he was big brother watching over her. It eventually became nursing a beer and watching the show. Out of his friendship for Luc he let it lie.

"I don't know what I could have done differently Danny, we needed the money, and I needed to focus on my studies. What could I have done for a different outcome?"

"You could've needed her...I think she might have loved you... I know she didn't love Animal, he was her boy toy, as were a few other guys hanging out there...I'm not sure if she did nor didn't, love's out of my league..."

"I hate baseball."

Relegated to the dugout, it was the only response Luc could muster in a cloud of smoke.

Labor Day

EIGHTEEN

To avoid having to sit through the chaos of a family fiesta, Francisco made the excuse Americanos hung out in bars over the holidays, and he needed to stay open. He also needed to take over for his son Hector who need to hit the books again. Truth be told, retirement for Francisco scared the hell out of him. He'd tend to business until his son graduated. He also knew no one would be dropping in on Labor Day, everyone was already out in their backyards drinking pisswater and roasting dogs. Except that is two regulars Luc and Danny. Francisco put his traditional toast on the bar. Luc put it to his nose, which given his state of exhaustion was not far from the glass.

"What is this…smells like nail polish?" He took a sip. "Tastes like smoke…or is it just me."

"The nail polish could be you amigo." Danny picked up the bottle. "It's Mezcal, and it does have a smoky taste." He passed the bottle over to Luc. "Take a gander at what's floating on the bottom, that'll be yours when we finish the bottle."

After pulling an all-nighter, leaving nothing to drink, to snort, or to smoke in the townhouse, Luc and

Danny had stopped for breakfast at Jaime's Hut. At this juncture he could not fathom eating a worm after having downed a bowl of menudo—a traditional remedy for hangovers made with unmentionable ingredients. Francisco poured three more shots.

"I usually save the worm for special occasions and you boys look like this is something special. Salud!"

"Francisco, what would you do if your wife left you for another man?"

"If it was you Danny I'd say the best of luck. But mi esposa…another man…where could she find someone better than me. I provide for her, and the niños, I give her a casa, she has running water, and an indoor toilet, and I love her cooking, what more could she want."

Francisco also knew when it came to beautiful women, married men wear horse blinders to prevent them from becoming distracted or panicked by what's around them.

"Have you ever known another women besides your wife Francisco? Ever thought about another women?"

Luc knew that in spite of his bravado Francisco was a faithful family man.

"If you tell me of a hombre who doesn't think about another woman he devours with his eyes, I tell you of someone who has already starved to death. I think you need to put on a little weight Luc."

"Sounds pretty profound for an old married man."

Luc ignored the weight line knowing that sitting in front of a microphone for hours on end had its drawbacks. He inched his glass toward Francisco for a refill. He liked this mezcal. The conversation turn to the situation he'd been trying to drown.

"So what did I do wrong Danny? For Christ sakes, I gave her two French poodles. Not as good as Francisco, maybe."

"I was with her when she bought the dogs. I don't recall she talked to you about them. I'm not one to explore relationships Luc, but I don't think you want to try and analyze to death what's happened. Write to Ann Landers and see what she has to say. I don't think you're going to get anywhere trying to figure this one out."

Danny's physical wound in Nam, and the underlining psychological dysfunction that followed prevented him from having a relationship with any women —so he thought. Living in his vehicle made it easy to avoid getting involved. He did, from a distance get involved with Colette. She was crazy fun. Had a wicked tongue in more ways than one. This, however, was not the time to talk to Luc about Colette. He'd already exhausted that subject.

"After forty years of marriage can you remember Francisco what it would be like to be with a young woman like Collette?" Danny moved the topic back over to Francisco.

"I have eyes don't I. I have been surrounded by beautiful señoritas all my life. You should be so lucky. There is a Mexican saying when times are bad put on a good face; *Al mal tiempo, buena cara.*"

He was making light of the situation to cheer Luc up. He refilled the shot glasses. Mezcal was going down too easy. He addressed Luc,

"If you have to abandon your casa, maybe you can park your burrow in Danny's casita in front of the cantina."

"Ain't gonna happen Francisco. He can't park his fat ass in the van. It's a high rent district in front of the Cantina. Plus no dogs allowed. Luc needs a part time job. You need a nighttime bartender, and then you can stay home at nights with your lovely señoritas. I think Luc would make a decent bartender, if he didn't drink all the profits. Attend classes during the day, serve drinks at night just like Hector. What do you think Luc?"

Francisco thought about Luc bartending. Not at La Cantina, he wasn't going anywhere, let alone home in the evenings.

"I have a better idea Luc. I've got a relative who's opening a night club on Dyer Street, just off the army base. He's married to mi esposa's-sister's-daughter. Plans to cater to the horny GIs. He's got this wild idea for what he calls a disco with male dancers attracting young women to come and drink. I could see if he needs a macho gringo bartender." He looked up at the coca cola clock on the back wall. "I give him a call if you're interested."

Danny nudged Luc, who responded by moving his glass toward the mezcal bottle.

"He's interested Francisco. The stud part attracting young women I'm sure he can handle. Don't know about the bar thing. Where's this guy hang out."

"He's familia. It's a holiday weekend. He's sure to be at mi casa eating my food and drinking my booze. It's why I'm here. I can tell them I still have customers and not tell a lie."

"There you are Luc, you got a job." Danny slapped Luc on the shoulder. "Now all you need to do is get rid of the dogs, the townhouse, the furniture, and the memory of your French coquette. Oh Yeh, and find a place to hang the hat you don't wear."

When Francisco hung up the phone and turned to the bar, Danny was holding up his glass.

"You in the market for a couple poodle dogs Francisco?"

"They're not dogs, they're chuchería. His name is Guillermo, my wife's-sister's-daughter's-husband, and he'll see Luc. He's to call him."

Francisco wrote Guillermo and his phone number on a piece of paper, and handed it to Danny.

"Luc perked up. "What's a chuchería Francisco?"

"You'd call it a gewgaw."

94

"Right. A plastic Jesus. I thought those dogs were called fish bait in Mexico."

The mezcal had kicked in and Luc was off in the ozone. Before the boys left La Cantina Francisco gave Danny a well-worn copy of Mr. Boston Official Bartenders Guide, and told him to have Luc study it. When Danny got him home safely, Luc asked him to bivouac in the townhouse until he figured out which way the wind's blowing. Danny agreed, it would be a place to dry dock his U.S. Navy Eagle P cap for a while. Before passing out Luc thought of Dylan's song, "Blowing in the Wind," and knew nothing out there was quite what it seemed to be.

NINETEEN

Guillermo's English was as unpolished as Luc's Spanish and it made for an interesting interview. Entering the building he was confronted with a dozen men with their equipment was scattered throughout a large empty hall. They were working on the floor, the walls, and all around a twenty foot mahogany bar while earsplitting decibels emanated from the Mexican radio station, playing what sounded to Luc as one conjunto norteño song over and over again; the sound of the tuba in beat with the hammers of the workmen, adding to the chaos of the moment. Guillermo, heavy set, unshaven, wearing a well-worn striped sharkskin rockabilly suit, paid more attention to the electrician installing a 24 inch mirrored disco ball than he did to Luc. His plan was to open Zippers the first week of October. The name Zippers, Guillermo explained carried with it sexual overtones, and would attract the female clientele. Luc could start the last week of September to help with the inventory and make sure the bar was ready. Guillermo took a cursory glance at the résumé; Francisco's recommendations were more than enough to land the job. He would start with Friday nights through Sunday nights, and to accommodate his school schedule he would only work a couple night shifts during the week. Luc's dubious skills as a bartender were secondary to what Guillermo needed behind the bar following Francisco advise, a stud gringo vet.

Now with a job all but sewed up, Luc was determined not to have to crash in Danny's van. Colette, having depleted their bank account for her escape, left Luc no choice but to make moving a primary task. Last month's rent was covered so he was off the hook for September's rent. The garage sale brought in enough to pay the phone bill and bankroll another abode. Luc had no luck at the garage sale finding a home for BamBam and Bubba. He didn't want them to end up in a puppy farm in Juarez, so he turned to Professor Irving's wife Dolores. She had taken to Luc over the last semester, and even better as it turned out, she loved poodles. The Irving's lost their only son Malcolm in Nam. He was a helicopter pilot shot down during the 1968 Tet offensive. She saw in Luc, who was the same age as Malcolm, some of the attributes her son had: thoughtful, positive, and independent. Talking her into taking the poodles—name change required, did not ingratiate him with the Professor, who had no desire to start a new family a couple years away from retirement. Unencumbered, it was imperative he now found a place before he began working. The answer to Luc's housing dilemma came when Danny met up with him at La Cantina. It came in a roundabout way with a surprise invitation to Albert Hogan and Angelica Garcia Chavez's wedding reception. Luc had not heard from Albert since the fateful visit when Kate's abduction was revealed. Their paths seldom crossed and Luc, still guilt ridden over his affair with Albert's wife, didn't go looking for a connection.

"Do you remember the first time we met at Albert's? It was out by the pool when Angel and Steve were there." Danny turned down Francisco's offer of tequila. "Just a Tecate, I'm driving." Parked outside the bar it was a familiar joke that didn't travel far. Tecate Mexico's poor man's cerveza had replaced Lone Star, the national beer of Texas as the drink of choice since Francisco returned from his belated honeymoon in Mexico City.

"I do. It was the first time I met up with Angel as well. A fateful encounter."

"The girl in the pool, do you remember her?"

"I don't recall her name, but I do remember her body. It was a chilly night and she was wearing a bikini. She was all goosebumps coming out of the pool."

"That's her, Angelica, Albert's bride to be. And those weren't big goosebumps. The wedding's tomorrow."

"Have you been staying in touch with Albert?"

"On occasion we'd get together for a beer, usually with Angel. He still lives in the same place, and his roommate is Angelica's brother. He's an army vet."

"What's Albert been doing all this time? I've never seen him on campus. Never had the opportunity to introduce him to Colette."

"Working on his Master's. Almost done, I think. He's still into playing the politician. He now speaks Spanish which helps because his fiancé is from the El Segundo Barrio, and their getting married in the El Sagrado Corazon Catholic Church."

"You're bullshitting me. Albert doesn't know what the inside of a church looks like." Luc recalled Albert trying to figure out what confessional, absolution, and annulment were all about."

"I guess he's been converted. The Catholics have the missionary roll down pat. They've been baptizing pagans around here since Don Juan de Oñate took possession of the Rio Grande."

Francisco and his familia had settled in El Segundo when they first came to El Paso from Boquillas. He attended The Sacred Heart Church, all his children were baptized there. He knew Albert getting married there would be a community event. He filled the boys in on the event.

"You're right Danny. Albert would have to become Catholic. Her parents would not let him marry their daughter if he wasn't. I know the family well. It will be a big wedding. Everybody will attend, everybody is welcome, including my family. Albert is marrying into *prominente* in the Barrio. He will have to seek La Pedida, her father's approval. As head of the household he has the final say when it comes to giving his daughter away. Alberto has no family here, he was most likely sponsored by someone of note in the community."

"Could be the Mayor, he's been working with him ever since he was a senior. Do you know anybody who might sponsor him Luc?"

"You'd know better than I would Danny. His family's long gone from here. Albert's the ultimate politician, he'll do whatever he needs to get elected; find a sponsor, become a catholic. Francisco we need to toast Albert."

Francisco filled three shot glasses with tequila, ignoring Danny's previous refusal. "Salud!"

When they placed their empty glasses on the bar, Luc continued. "Tell me about El Segundo Francisco, I know it's just south of here. I've driven through there but I haven't paid much attention."

"Most gringos stay clear of the Barrio Luc, its 99.9% Mexican. Albert's the .1% exception. The second ward is one of the oldest neighborhoods in El Paso. It is where Mexicans have settled since the late 1800s. As a demographic it is considered one of poorest communities in the U.S., and a staging ground for those able to go north. Until the 60s there were no paved streets, and no street lights. It borders the Rio Grande going east where it becomes farmland. El Sagrado Corazon, was built by the Jesuits in 1893, and is the oldest church in El Paso."

"Albert having a Mexican church wedding, I wouldn't have bet on it. Danny, I think we should attend.

"If you boys attend be prepared for a long service, lots of standing, sitting, and kneeling. It will be a traditional Mexican *boda*."

"Who's paying for all this Francisco? Albert's a student, probably still on a scholarship."

"No hay problema Luc, Albert is mucho lucky. It is customary in traditional weddings the father of the bride will pay the expenses, and the padrinos and madrinos, or godparents, will help financially."

"Go figure. Albert will probably be running for office in the second ward before long. Another toast Francisco."

Francisco topped up the glasses.

"*Al que ha de ser charro, del cielo le cae el sombrero*, he cannot walk away from his destiny. Salud!"

TWENTY

It wasn't even close to resembling the first and only Mexican wedding Luc had been invited to. In Dallas, he attended his friends Carlos and Felicita's traditional wedding. It was an intimate gathering of family and friends in St. Anne's Church, followed by a hot and spicy feast in their backyard, accompanied by mariachis. This one was a community event and a gathering of generations. The Sacred Heart Church was filled to the rafters. The service was already in progress when Luc and Danny arrived on the scene. It was standing room only at the back, which suited them since it was high mass and high fashion, and they looked just a little out of place as usual. The bride and groom, 'novia y el novio' as Francisco called them, and their attendants were standing at the Church's alter. Albert was wearing a white tux with a *guayabera*, a traditional Mexican wedding shirt. Angelica was wearing a *vestido de novia* and *a mantilla* style veil. Francisco had told them she most likely would have three ribbons sewn into her lingerie for good luck—yellow, blue, and red, meant to ensure, plenty of food, money, and passion. After the exchange of vows the couple were lassoed together with a long strand of rosary beads, wrapped around their shoulders in a figure eight, and stayed tied together through the rest of the service. Francisco said it happened to him during his wedding, and after he was lassoed and hogtied his wife didn't untie the noose.

The reception commenced immediately after the ceremony on the grounds of the church, and was open to anyone in the barrio who could find a place to sit and dance. The mariachis were dressed in their black and white charro costumes, the concrete dance floor was awash in color and gyrating bodies, and of course the *comida y bebida en abundancia*. Luc and Danny no sooner grabbed a table when Steve and Angel joined them.

"Steve, Angel, thought you guys would be around somewhere. Pull up a chair, they'll be few and far between in a short time."

Angel didn't sit down. He was ready to party. Steve pulled up a chair.

"Come on Danny, let's get some refreshments while the beers cold."

Steve was dressed as dapper as the first time Luc met him; this time a sport coat with western yokes and embroidered arrows, alligator boots and Stetson hat.

"Are you in town just for the wedding?" Last Luc knew he graduated and move east.

"Yeh I'm still in Austin working on my law degree. Staying with Albert and his roommate Alejandro at the apartment while I'm here. Have to head back tomorrow. And you?"

"Working on my senior year. What do you know about Albert's roommate?"

"Alejandro, he's Albert's best man. Couldn't miss him at the altar, he's one of the few Hispanics over 6 feet."

"How long has he been living with Albert?"

"Since Steve left for law school I thing. Not for long though. After the honeymoon, a friend of the family has set the newlyweds up in a condo in Puerto Vallarta, then they'll be moving into a house in the Barrio compliments of Angelica's grandfather."

"Nice work if you can get it.

Danny and Angel returned with armfuls of beer.

"It's musica, cerveza, and comida for the rest of the afternoon; speeches will come later when everyone's satiated. Angel suggested we stock up on essentials."

Danny dropped his load on the table. It was well into the afternoon before Albert could make it to their table, and it was handshakes and back slaps all around.

"Hola Amigos, sorry it took this long. One has to hug and kiss all the women, it's tradition. I can't hang out for long, we're getting to where we start the speeches."

"It'll all be in Spanish, can you handle it?"

"The secret Luc is to keep smiling and pretend everything said is a compliment. Plus, I've learned a helluva lot of Spanish during my pillow talks with Angelica."

Standing beside Albert was a tall, muscular Hispanic wearing a peasant shirt and Levis. Everybody at the table knew him except Luc. Over the load speaker someone was calling for el novio.

"Sounds like they're after you Albert. Time for the dog and pony show. I'll see if I can find you a chair Alejandro." Angel stood up and looked around.

"Luc, meet Alejandro Garcia Chavez, the one and only brother of Angelica. Danny tells me you might be looking for a place to hang out at, and Alejandro is minus a roommate as of tonight. Catch you guys later, looks like I'm in demand." Albert turned and danced, sort of, across the yard.

Luc stood up and shook Alejandro's hand. "Nice to meet you. Albert's right, I am in the market for a place. Let's see if we can find you a chair. Any luck Angel?"

"Nada, standing room only."

"Thanks but I'm not staying. Did my part as best man. It's been nonstop wedding for the last few days, and for someone who doesn't like crowds, I should get a medal

103

for this one. I'll be at the apartment the rest of the day, or tomorrow if you want to drop by.

"I think Danny and I are busting out soon. Once the speeches start, unless Angel or Steve want to translate. Feel like stopping over, Danny."

"No hay problema. Best go while we're still standing."

For Steve and Angel, the party was just starting and probably wouldn't end until early mañana.

For an ex Special Forces sharp shooter, surviving two deployments in Nam, Alejandro had all the attributes of a gentle giant: laid back, quiet demeanor, easy going. No one knew what he'd been through in the war, he never spoke to anyone about it, with one exception being Danny. Danny carried the physical scars, Alejandro the mental. On the drive over to the apartment Danny gave Luc a taste of what he knew.

"When Alejandro was discharged upon returning to the States he was all fucked up. He scored a supply of yellow sunshine acid and headed for the Sierra Madres. Don't know how long until he surfaced, could have been a year. He returned to El Paso all mellowed out. I met him in rehabilitation at the Vets Hospital when I was recovering. He's also attending university on the GI bill."

"What's his major?"

"Criminal Justice. Albert got to know him when Steve invited him to one of the Friday night gigs. Angelica who'd been there once before with a girlfriend joined him. The rest is history."

"When did all this take place?" Luc flashed on Kate.

"Rehabilitation was at the Vet Center a couple years ago. He's been laying low living at home in the Barrio. We were still doing the Friday night gig up until Albert got heavy into his Master's, and Angelica finally had him pussy whipped."

Luc didn't know how much Alejandro knew about Colette riding off with Animal, but considering Danny was the Walter Winchell of gossip he didn't have to ask. He moved in the weekend before he started work at Zippers. Alejandro worked at a flower shop right off campus, and told him if he didn't want to bartend he could get a job there, they were looking for a driver, and he could work around his schedule. Sometimes life gives you a walk in the garden to make a decision, Luc chose to go for the money, and let it unfold as it may. A formula he knew, was tumbleweed blowing in the wind.

TWENTY-ONE

The Franklin Mountains paralleled Dyer Street on the west, and to the east of Dyer a military base occupied a flat, very flat seventeen hundred square miles of desert. Fort Bliss, one of the largest army training grounds in North America, since the 1800s provided a sizeable economic impact on El Paso. After spending time in Dallas disco clubs, Guillermo, Francisco's wife's-sister's-daughter's-husband figured two things would have an positive economic impact on his wallet by opening a nightclub next to Fort Bliss. First off the drinking age in Texas was recently lowered from 21 to 18, letting loose on the streets a shitload of young buck soldiers with money to spend. The second was the emergence of disco music. This combination lead to his brilliant idea of creating a disco club catering to young Hispanic women, who in turn would attract the GIs like bees to honey. Luc didn't know how the two came together, but Guillermo was gung ho. Since the Vietnam War's winding down, Luc surmised the bored army grunts would be looking for another place to wear off some testerone. Guillermo named the club Zippers, which didn't translate well into Spanish, cremalleras, but for him it seemed to have some lower body inference he thought might relate to his future clientele. His new boss had a weird Mexican sense of humor, and for Luc it was somewhere on the other side of the cultural divide. As was the Luc's uniform of the day, a cross between cowboy and stud; hip hugging bell bottoms and a silk white shirt open down to the *ombligo* showing off his hairy chest, all topped off with a white Stetson. Guillermo was replicating everything he saw in Dallas, a day's drive from El Paso, and to some not just another time zone, another planet.

The week prior to opening Zippers, Luc had the opportunity to practice for the expected onslaught of alcoholic drinks he'd have to serve. Since he was a beer, tequila, and straight Jack Daniels consumer, with the very occasional mezcal, his personal repertoire when it came to mixed drinks was limited. Danny, Francisco, joined by Alejandro, in the week before grand opening held evening classes at La Cantina, utilizing Luc's text book, Old Boston. Mr. Boston's Official Bartender's Guide was now a constant companion. He was ready when the club opened with the book dog eared for long island iced tea, fuzzy navels, brown cows, melon balls, and black and white Russians. Guillermo's opening party with amigos y familia as invited guests went well, thanks in part to the free booze. After a couple hours of the Gloria Gaynor, Kool & The Gang, Barry White, and Carl Douglas, by the time KC & The Sunshine Band broke the sound barrier with "Do It Good," any familia over thirty was good to go, never to return. Guillermo scored his disco playlist from his connections in Dallas. He was soon to discover he was introducing music foreign to the ears of all but a few.

The rest of the week was a bust. Guillermo ran ads in the Fort Bliss Bugle, and the El Paso Herald-Post. For the few Hispanic and Anglo women who ventured in, it was cerveza and giggles at the two Hispanic male waiters who doubled as dancers, in their scant attire. For the young military grunts who sat at the bar staring at an empty dance floor, lit only by the sixteen inch mirror disco ball, Guillermo's pride and joy, conversation was limited due to the incessant four-on-the-floor beat of disco music, pounding the eardrums. In Dallas spandex tops with hot pants were just becoming the staple disco wear for women, a fashion the Southwest was not quite ready for. The GI's wearing their wrinkled mufti didn't add to the atmosphere Guillermo envisioned.

It didn't get any better. Disco required a dedicated kinetic sweaty mayhem on the dance floor, and it would take a major shift for the beat to break through the culture of Cumbia, and Tejano. The young soldiers were ready to march to the beat, except males dancing with one another was another cultural barrier, and it didn't bode well at Zippers. Guillermo soon let the backup bar help go for lack of business, they were down to one waiter/dancer, and Luc found himself pulling a weight he wasn't expecting. He was working Monday to Saturday, and three weeks into the grand adventure, Guillermo was running low on finances. Luc was running low on balancing school work and bar work.

Danny became a regular, occupying a bar stool to keep his buddy company. It was Halloween, and the following Monday was the beginning of exam week, when Angel joined Danny at the bar.

"Impressive costume Luc." It was Angel's first visit.

Luc was wearing a Groucho Marx glasses, nose, and moustache mask.

"I haven't worn a costume since my army uniform. Guillermo insisted I do something. The lime green hippie ball busting bell bottom pants for the dancers was his idea as well. He added another waiter for event."

There was one table with 5 GIs drinking shots of tequila and chasing them with Coors. The two tables with couples drinking beer and Long Island Iced Tea, only cracked the dance floor when the Supremes played. It was a rare busy night, and having started up on a hope and a promise, if nothing changed by Thanksgiving Guillermo might be looking at running out of reserve capital. Luc barely made the grade on his mid-terms. Things were shaky all around. Guillermo gave it until the second week into November before sitting down at the bar and ordering a brandy sour. It was Friday night and the club was empty. It was Luc's first brandy sour, and a recipe, if it's too sour, undrinkable. Guillermo took one sip, puckered, and ordered Jack Daniels straight.

"Sorry boss, I followed Old Boston. Should have been okay."

"Have you seen Francisco lately?"

"Not lately, I've been too busy to hang out at La Cantina. Danny hangs out there and he tells me Francisco's been concerned about Zipper's not performing as expected. How he knows I don't know."

He filled Guillermo's glass. Luc made it a point not to drink while on the job, at least when the boss was around, and so far so good.

"He's padre, he knows. There are no secrets when it comes to Francisco."

Guillermo nursed his glass of whiskey, and tried to convince himself of what he was about to say. How to make a success out of a bar in El Paso unless it came with a house Mariachi, Norteño, and Banda band, obviously required a bigger bankroll or a magical gimmick.

"I have to make some changes. I've talked to my compadres in Dallas, and they agree this idea of a heterosexual disco bar is ahead of its time. It works in Dallas, but they think it'll take a couple years to reach El Paso."

"Why do you think that is?"

"I know why it is. It's the fucking Catholic mentality." Guillermo made the sign of the cross. "It's got

Mexican women brainwashed. They don't know how to get together, go out and kick up some shit without a chaperone."

"I think Dallas has got it right, you're just ahead of your time. Got to be a big cultural leap for young Hispanic virgins to go out at night without a male guardian. I think you got the right idea with the disco music though. It's time is coming." Luc was trying to be conciliatory.

Guillermo scanned the empty dance floor. There was one waiter on shift who was sitting at the far end of the bar. He leaned over the bar, and lowered his voice. It was not as if anyone in the club, even if there was someone at a table, could hear him over the beat of the music.

"How do you feel about homosexuals?"

This was a question Luc had to search for the appropriate answer. He wasn't sure what Guillermo was asking given his macho man persona.

"I've a couple friends who are gay, it's never been an issue with me." Luc had no idea where his boss was going with this.

"I've been thinking if we're going to survive this club needs new clientele. My friends in Dallas says the homos love disco, love to party and drink. They think Zippers might be a name they're attracted to. What about the GIs, think they would be interest?"

Where that leap in logic came from Luc left alone.

"Maybe we can accommodate all the closet gays hanging out in the latrines on Fort Bliss. I think foxhole might be a better term than closet. I guess you've done your homework boss. How do you get the word out? I don't think you can advertise a gay friendly night club in the Herald-Post, or on base."

"I'm hoping word of mouth." He turned his head away from the staff member at the end of the bar and lowered his voice another decibel. "I suspect the male dancers we hired might be gay, don't you think, they could spread the word."

"It won't be nubile senoritas, any longer, not as if it ever has been, but you still might have a place for ladies of the night."

Luc was thinking about David's crowd. From what he had learned there was a good size subculture below the radar in El Paso and Juarez.

"If it doesn't fly I may be selling tacos on the street corner." Guillermo was searching for a solution.

The word of mouth turned out not to be David but did happened to be the Lady of the Night in El Paso's gay community. Queen Vulvalita, drag queen extraordinaire, with thick painted lips that would make a blowfish jealous, inch long eyelashes framed by an overabundance of eye shadow, all tucked under a psychedelic purple wig the size of a cornucopia Easter bonnet. There were only a couple tables of GI's drinking beer when she arrived Friday evening, Thanksgiving weekend. The soldiers closest to the exit went AWOL, or as Danny phrased it, the trench monkeys have gone Elvis. She swished in, all feathers, a firefly, playing the room like a multi-colored pinball, and when the gay entourage she brought with her swarmed the bar and the dance floor the few remaining GIs left their money on the table and headed for the foxholes. Guillermo, holed up in his office for several days came out and stood in the doorway. Vulvalita landed on a bar stool next to Danny.

"Are you one of the brave testeroneee boys from the base?"

Danny looked at Luc standing behind the bar for support, and turning back to Vulvalita. "Actually I'm…"

She cut him off giving Luc a once over.

"Oh my, were have you been hiding." She turned and waved her feathers at her train and shouted above the music. "This dear boy is going to make us all margaritas. Are we game?" There was a chorus of arms flailing to

"Kung Fu Fighting."

"I guess it's a yes. Danny can you help me with this one? Don't want our guests getting thirsty."

Danny was all too quick to get behind the bar.

"Queen Velvulita." She leaned across the bar with her arm extended. "And you are?"

"It's a pleasure to meet you." He reached over and touched her elbow length black satin glove. "I'm Luc, I live here when I'm not sleeping."

"Shame. Do you sleep alone?"

"Not if I can help it."

"This has the makings of a promising relationship. I'm looking for the name Guillermo. I here tell thru the grapevine he's in need of some refreshing clientele."

"That would be the gentleman hiding in the doorway at the far end of the dance floor. He owns the place."

Danny fast tracked a margarita using premade mix and put it on the bar.

"Well then, I'll just take my drink and introduce myself. Don't you go away sweet thing." She took a small brown vial from her purse and put it on the bar. "This is for you girls, a house warming gift."

Luc turned to help Danny who had lined up nine salted glasses and with margarita mix in one hand was pouring in a hefty amount of tequila with the other.

"What'd think is in the brown bottle Danny?"

"It's amyl nitrite. Must be for us, I don't think they need it, their all pretty euphoric."

Queen Vulvalita remained with Guillermo until the 'girls' as she referred to the gyrating bodies on the dance floor, swinishly downed their margaritas, and gyrated to the front door leaving their empty glasses on the table next to the exit. Seems this was a one stop quickie on their Friday night junket. When she flew out of Guillermo's office she blew Luc a kiss and led her entourage into the night.

Guillermo sat down at the bar and asked for a whiskey.

"Put his," he hesitated, "her tab on my account Luc. Complimentary drinks for new customers. What gives with the brown bottle? He picked it up, sniffed it, and nearly fell off the bar stool. "Jesus!" He straightened up and made the sign of the cross.

Luc and Danny sensed change in the air.

TWENTY-TWO

The Pet Shop in downtown El Paso already catered to lesbians, El Buen Tiempo Cantina in Ciudad Juárez was the playground for gay cowboys, Zippers just added to the mix. Forever looking for a place to perform Queen Vulvalita adopted Zippers, and took Luc under her wings. As ringleader, a visit to Zippers did not go by without trying to get Luc to join the circus. For Luc bartending was now what he thought it might be, nonstop crazy, and a whole lot of fun. Guillermo hired more waiters and let the dancers go solo. They had no problem skimping down on the dress code, which no longer existed, and their tips kept them moving with the beat. He lowered the lights and raised the volume, the music a combination of nonstop funk, soul and ever more popular disco. When he learned straight males came to the club to look for young Guillermo's or Guillermo Latino's for sex in the washroom, he announced he was changing his handle to his nickname Chuy.

Danny, Angel and Alejandro became regular attendees at the bar. They came to watch the show on a dance floor covered in shaking boodies. Blow, Quaaludes, and the latest drug enhanced the dance floor experience of pounding base and the hypnotic light from the disco ball, and gave Angel a thriving new market. After providing Luc with little brown bottles of locker room, amyl nitrite became a staple along the bar. It was a prescription drug Luc was first briefly introduced to by professor's Oliver and Gordon during his Alpine days at Big Bend University. Not for their heart conditions, nor for the sexual arousal and desire it brought on, they liked the buzz poppers gave them. Sniffing locker room gave a burst of euphoric energy with a rush of blood to the brain and heart, catapulting users back onto the dance floor.

Luc's bartending skills were tested to the max with fuzzy navels, mind erasers, orgasms, long slongs, and woo woos. He gave up the hairy chest and bell bottoms for tee-shirts and tight jeans, and was hit on every night from an audacious onslaught of after-hours party goers. After Zippers turned on the lights, and shut the doors, there were all night venues downtown, and in Juarez where border fags and dykes, Anglos, Mexicans, and whatever reveled in drag shows, foam parties, and military nights. Luc fought off the temptation to party hearty until the Saturday night following final exams, when an unexpected meeting up with an old friend launched the Holiday Season.

Danny hung out at the club periodically when it was Chuy's attempt at a straight disco, mainly to keep Luc company. Once the club came out of the closet Danny, with his Texas Baptist background was back to hanging out at La Cantina. He had no bias towards the gay scene, his comfort zone was based on preconditioning, Francisco, on the other hand, was fit to be tied over his wife's-sister's-daughter's-hombre's decision.

Alejandro took Danny's place, and made Zippers a regular Friday and Saturday night gig, staying until Luc closed. He sat at the far end of the bar, away from the dance floor and nursed a beer. He didn't mingle or make friends, and Luc figured his roommate just enjoyed the circus. When things got crazier than normal he'd help out behind the bar. He was covering for Luc, who had gone to the water closet, when a tall, athletic man sat down on bar stool across from him. Alejandro ignored the waiter calling in his order at the end of the bar.

"What's your pleasure?"

"What cognac do you carry?"

Alejandro wasn't sure Zippers carried cognac. He turned and scanned the liquor shelves.

"The only one is Courvoisier."

"Perfect."

Luc stepped up behind the customer. "Make it a double Alejandro. If I recall Lee your preference used to be Old Fashions."

Lee swirled and slid off the bar stool. Hugging was appropriate in Zippers. "

Old Fashions were just that, they got old. No, I switched to cognac after moving in with Morris."

Alejandro put Lee's drink on the bar and reluctantly gave in to the impatient onslaught of waiters.

Luc stepped back to take a good look.

"You haven't change a bit Lee. You're still as handsome as ever. What brings you to Zippers of all places?"

"I'm still gay. I've managed to avoid aversion therapy. Just stopping off on my way to California, and heard about this place. And you, what are you doing here? Have you finally abandoned those ancient heterosexual tendencies?

"It's a long story, but no, still madly in love with the opposite sex, although it's not exactly working up to my expectations at the moment. And where might DeBone be in the scheme of things, and Rosey, Robert?"

"Morris died of a heart attack. Too much of the good life. Rosey's latched on to a new ride. She's doing okay, taking Granny to church every Sunday. Robert bought a membership at the golf club, last I heard he was going to run for some kind of office. Go figure.

"Everything changes, and then again as Allison pointed out, nothing ever really changes under the magnolias.

"I went back to Arkansas after the funeral. I landed a temporary teaching position at Henderson College, and managed to maintain my teaching qualifications." It just felt like I was in another closet, and when Morris died, you know. Nothing there anymore but memories, some good, some not worth remembering. The Professor and Roberto have a thing going other than that. Thought I'd head out to Santa Monica to see what cousin Tex is up to and check out the schools there. Financially I'm not in a hurry to settle down where I'm not welcome. It's still a wild and crazy gay world out there on the coast.

"If I remember you were heading out to the west coast once before, and East Texas was as far as you got. Are you up to a night on the town? You can crash at our place as long as you want."

"The clocks not ticking. Who's the 'our' in our place."

Luc motioned Alejandro over. "Like you to meet my roommate Alejandro. Helps me out at the bar occasionally. Alejandro come and keep Lee company while I get back to earning a paycheck, he's going to be our guest for as long as we can hijack him."

TWENTY-THREE

Juarez, with a little imagination could be compared to Las Vegas; open for business twenty four hours a day, and it was an adult playground, stimulated by drugs, booze, and sex—it just lacked the lights, the glamor, and the glitter. Most of what a countless number of GI's, and the El Paso High school kids crossed the International Bridge for was down dark alleys, behind partially closed doors guarded by savory looking characters, down dark alleys, in basement caverns awash with spilt booze, and earsplitting attempt at music. Juarez was also the wild and wooly west for the alternative night life.

Queen Vulvalita's persona of Judy Garland, was the highlight of the drag shows, along with Marilyn Monroe, Marlene Dietrich, and the Brazilian Bombshell Carmen Miranda. It was harmless raunchy fun, and it all lit up the night. At a bathhouse, one of many popular Juarez saturnalian naked pursuits, Alejandro's coming out, a cause of uninhibited celebration, convinced Lee to hang around for the Holidays. Upon reflection, Luc was not surprised, there was a reason Alejandro hung out at Zippers, and the reason he had not fallen for the army of eligible Mexican daughters his family had thrown at him. Individual preferences outside of perversion and bigotry no longer made an impression on Luc. It was civil twilight when the trio stumbled across the International Bridge and found Lee's car in a parking lot off Stanton Street. They were fortunate it was still there, having left it unlocked. Alejandro was the designated driver only because he was the one who after a lengthy search found the keys thrown under the driver's seat.

Zippers slowed to a crawl over the holidays giving Luc plenty of time to sit behind the bar and read. He'd given up on Christmas a long time ago, there were few positive or negative memories to hang onto. Chuy gave the staff ample time off, and he was all familia leaving the club to Luc to manage. Nobody showed up at Zippers, the week between Christmas and New Year's, which meant sending the skeleton staff home early, locking up, turning down the lights, and killing the music. Luc sat at the bar drinking cognac, and reflecting on the cards he'd been dealt. Life used to be a pinochle game with a fistful of cards from two decks, now it was down to 5 card stud, and he didn't feel he was holding a winning hand. Lee had decided to stick around over the holidays and play with Alejandro. They reminded him of what he didn't have, a relationship with someone he could share the moment with. He was close to graduating, with a job covering the basics to survive, a place to hang out with all the comforts of home, and considering his penchant for reclusiveness, a few close friends. He couldn't put a finger on what he was missing, but he knew there was this hole in his life he wasn't digging out of. Every time he got close to the surface and the sun was in his face, it turned cloudy and began to rain. He was living in the Southwest desert where rain was a blessing, for Luc it was a curse. He could hide behind the bar with a packed house, and no one would notice how lonely he was inside.

During the New Year's Eve blowout at Zippers, the two new ladies of the night announced they were running off to Santa Monica together. Alejandro graduated in December, and she was footloose and fancy free. The she in he broke free, and with Lee, Alejandro could abandon the confines of an uncomfortable barrio of birth he had been trapped in all his life. Chuy was temporarily back in charge at the club, but stayed in his office ignoring the bacchanalian festivities. For New Year's he charged a buck a head at the door, offered free champagne and enough pizza to feed Fort Bliss. Bottles of locker room lined the bar. Danny brought along three of his classmates: Caledonia, Miranda, and Sallie, student nurses ready to party. It was the first time Luc saw Angel with a companion. She was a tall, slim Hispanic woman, and alongside short and stocky Angel, they reminded Luc of Mutt and Jeff. Zippers was closed New Year's Day, and staff were paid double time to come in and help Chuy clean up the mess if they were able to walk.

For Luc the first of the year was a day off, and as he watched Lee drive off, heading to California with Alejandro beside him, he had no idea if his roommate would return. He was making decent money at Zippers, and January's rent was paid up. The new year promised to be a better year, and maybe he'd meet someone to share time with, all work and no play was getting old. If it wasn't for the fact his goal when discharged from the army, a BA with a story to tell was within his grasp, he might be sitting in the backseat of Lee's Bonneville on his way to another chapter.

TWENTY-FOUR

When he arrived back at the club to set up the bar before opening he was walking tall in his polished Justins; after years of wear and tear, new heels and soles were his Christmas present to himself. He passed two Mexican men sitting at one of the tables adjacent to the bar. He assumed Chuy, whose silhouette he could see through the tinted glass windows in his office let them in. When Luc walked by they didn't acknowledge his presence. They were focused on the office. Luc opened up the cash and set up the condiments, cut the fruit, and wiped down the bar. He did not expect any clientele soon, they were generally nonexistent during the afternoon. The rest of the staff would be filtering in when darkness was setting in, closer to 4:30-5. Luc could make out Chuy pacing in front of his desk holding the telephone in one hand and swatting the air with the other.

When he stopped with the prep Luc walked over to the table where the two Mexican men were honed in on the office. Both were wearing matching blue and black pinstripe double breasted 2 pc suits, with six buttons and wide labels. Luc noticed both were wearing shiny black and white wingtip shoes. They reminded him of an Al Capone movie. Neither looked up from under their fedoras and didn't acknowledge when asked if they wanted something to drink. Luc shrugged and returned to the bar.

Guillermo's feeble attempt to attract young Hispanic women to enjoy the pleasures of a male body gyrating to the disco beat while perched on a wooden box, attempting to seduce sweet bees to honey, had gone over like the proverbial lead balloon, and it meant he had to reinvent Zippers or he going under. He felt he was leading edge with the Disco, and as for the switch to the gay scene, what could possibly go wrong. Francisco was the only one in his familia who knew what Zippers evolved into, and the secret was safe with him. Guillermo was raking in the profits moving into the new year. His success financially, however, did bring another 'family' to the table.

There was already a blossoming alternative club scene on both sides of the border, and the Mexican Mafia had its fingers in the till. Guillermo, having ignored the expected protocol, the two gentlemen were waiting on his decision to pay to play or bear the consequences. To play required a sizeable down payment to offset any unexpected ramifications from not accepting the offer he couldn't refuse. It was an unexpected time of reckoning to become a manager of a business he would no longer control. After he was on the phone for several hours talking to his compadres in Dallas, Guillermo bailed, more from fear than failure. The Godfather Part 2 was a hit at the box office. The Dallas suggestion for Guillermo, under the circumstances, was don't let the door hit ya where the good Lord split ya.

Francisco couldn't be more apologético for having referred Luc to his wife's-sister's-daughter's-estúpido husband. Both for the failed business, and for the den of iniquity in his observation, it turned into. Luc was sitting at the bar in La Cantina nursing a beer when Danny sat down beside him.

"Looks to me you could use a joint. Francisco told me about Zippers suddenly closing down. Too bad, I'm sure it was fun while it lasted."

Francisco put a beer down in front of Danny. "You call it fun. That *pendejo* Guillermo, if his wife ever found out what he was doing, have mercy on him. *Cría cuervos y te sacarán los ojos,* he knew if he bred crows they'd pluck out his eyes."

Francisco went off to serve a patron. It was Saturday night and the bar was actually busy. With classes starting in two weeks students were returning.

"I'll pass on the joint right now. It'd only take me down lower than I am. What's a pendejo?"

"Something similar to dick head, or stupid ass, take your pick."

They sat quietly watching Francisco hustle in and out from behind the bar. There was something on Danny's mind he'd been playing with for a couple days. It would mean a change in lifestyle, and maybe it was time. He didn't have the courage to wing it alone, but with Luc's sudden change of fortune, or misfortune, maybe he'd be interested.

"Luc, I've been thinking lately, like you I'm looking at graduating this semester and I need to rejoin civilization. This Nam problem will be hanging over my head for the rest of my life. I can now live with what came down, shit happens. I ran across this place in East El Paso off Copia Street. It's the tallest building in the area, 5 stories. It used to be a Brew House. I think it dates back to the 1800s. Anyway, the top floor of a two story attachment is for rent, three bedrooms, and a great view with a rooftop backyard overlooking a huge produce complex. Cheap, real cheap. Thinking maybe you might be interested in both moving up and downgrading now you're out of work, and your roommate Alejandro's run off to a life of sin and surf in California." Danny called across the bar, "Francisco, do you know anything about the Brew House, I'm thinking of renting there?"

Francisco put a beer on the bar for Luc and picked up his empty.

"I know the place well, my brother worked there when he was much younger, and mi padre sold the beer they brewed there for years. Mitchell's Special Lager it was popular all over Texas. Falstaff took over in the mid-fifties, and mi padre refused to carry what they claimed was beer. On Piedras Street, right down from where you'd be living there's Jaime's Hut, open 24 hours a day, best menudo in El Paso. I recall you two went there for their hangover remedy."

Luc knew for Danny parking the van, and taking up structural residency was a big step. Danny didn't mention his budding involvement with a healthy senior at UTEP was possibly the impetus behind the move. The reality of living off the GI bill again had not yet set in for Luc, but soon he couldn't afford to live in the apartment complex, and he wasn't sure how long it would take him to find work, again. It was déjà vu all over again, and it was getting annoyingly repetitive.

"I'm game if you are Danny. Right now, outside of graduating I'm just a tumbleweed blowing in the wind, or as I'm feeling like lately, driftwood washed up on shore waiting to be pulled back into the sea with the next storm. When and how do you want to make the move?"

"Now is as good as ever. I talked to the realtor, he has a for rent sign at the Vet Center. He said it's mine if I want to move in."

"Bueno Danny, you gonna like living on dry land. We need to celebrate your new casa." Francisco put a bottle of Sauza and three glasses on the bar. "*Más vale pájaro en mano que ciento volando*. Salud!"

The natives were restless in the cantina, and Francisco returned to tending tables without imbibing.

"I give up, what'd he say?"

"I'm not sure, but I think it was something about a bird in the hand or the bush." Danny was working on his Spanish.

When Francisco returned to the bar and poured a shot of tequila for himself, he looked tired.

"Glad you left a little for me, I was worried."

"I know you have plenty more hidden behind the bar. Why don't you hire some help and get to renew your role as *jefe de familia* to your wife and grandchildren. Luc here is an unemployed bartender who needs a job."

"You make me feel guilty Danny. If it wasn't for imbécil Guillermo, Luc would still be working and able to finish his school."

After downing his tequila, he looked around, the patrons were slowly beginning to filter back into the night. It would still be a couple hours before he cleaned up, closed down, and went home.

"Maybe you're right Danny. I have eleven nietos I don't even know their names. He topped up the glasses. "How would you feel about working on the weekends here Luc? It's not the fancy drinks you make in the night club, and the tips suck. Mi esposa will love you until she gets tired of me hanging around, again."

TWENTY-FIVE

The Falstaff Company purchased the Mitchell Brewing Company in 1956, and discontinued Mitchel's Special Lager, and the line of brands Mitchell's carried since the thirties. Falstaff began brewing their own brands until shutting down in 1967. The only living space available was a structure on the roof of an attached garage. In the living area there were three rooms big enough they could be used as bedrooms, a large space for entertaining, and an open kitchen area with the only pieces of furniture, a round wooden spool table with eight chairs. No shower, but a large claw foot tub. The Goodwill was not too far away and a place they could scrounge for furniture. Once the arachnids, scorpions and unidentifiable bugs were swept away it became a habitable space. A huge swamp cooler tempered the kitchen and dropped the temperature by around twenty degrees. For a few hundred a month, for a couple students, it was perfect, and private. The back area overlooked the huge fenced in El Paso Produce Company with rows of stalls serving the areas commercial businesses. It was a pantry for fresh fruit and vegetables, and they could just walk down the stairs to do their grocery shopping. They needed keys to the fence surrounding the whole complex and after hours, when the produce market closed, they were isolated. With no neighbors within earshot, privacy reined quiet. It was the calm before the storm.

Their first visitors came as a surprise when Luc working his weekend shift at La Cantina, Alejandro and Lee dropped in on their way through El Paso. Alejandro needed to pick up the few things he left at the apartment, Luc had transferred to their new residency, after that they were heading to Dallas, and Arkansas to collect what Lee had in storage. They had purchased a residence overlooking the Pacific. The real surprise came when they announced they were living together as a wedded couple. Not legal anywhere in the States, but the possibility of registering as a domestic partnership was at least talked about in California. For all intents and purposes, and fuck the government, they considered themselves now married— interracially to add spice to the mix.

This called for the first party at the brewery. It lasted several days, and proved to be Danny's coming out as well, just not in the biblical sense as Lee and Alejandro had done. His lifestyle for the last few years was not exactly conducive to courting the opposite sex, or any sex. Now having a roof over his head for a couple weeks, he was compelled to explore the possibility that some of his female classmates might want to participate in what he described as a belated moving in party. He was the only male in his class of budding nurses, and Sallie, Miranda, and Caledonia took him up on the offer to come and let their hair down. Angel, not to be left out when it came to party time, was there to provide the brain food. Queen Vulvalita, upon hearing it was not only a moving in party, it would be a belated gay wedding reception, brought along a troupe of feathers and ice cream. Both Danny and Luc blew off their Monday and Tuesday classes, and the workers in

127

the produce yard were entertained with the rooftop antics of Tlazolteotl, Aztec goddess of carnality, and sexual misdeeds.

Luc knew the party scene was a dangerous road to go down, especially during his last semester, with all the signposts pointing to graduation. He managed since the fateful Resurrection and Abduction, with Nurse Danny's help maintain a semblance of sobriety with only a few blips by keeping one foot firmly on the ground, and at the very least avoiding things that would kill him. His goal of graduating was within his reach, however, personally it was a repeat of dead ends when it came to something he could hold onto, something he could claim was worth the trip. Now, going through the motions with his courses, and his weekend work, getting high was again routine to numb the senses. Danny, on the other hand, trapped for years in a mindset he was no longer capable physically of maintaining a relationship with the opposite sex, was adding a chapter to the bestselling Joy of Sex. As it turned out the three student nurses he previously invited to the New Year's party exhibited few inhibitions, and the fallout from Nam was no challenge.

Luc was tending bar when Lee and Alejandro stopped in at La Cantina having loaded the Bonneville and towing a U-Haul on their way back to Santa Monica.

"Sorry, no Courvoisier today. We've got a bottle of Presidente Brandy. Our esteemed patrons mix it with coca cola."

"I'll pass. How about two Tecates with lime and salt." Lee pulled up a bar stool, Alejandro sat in between him and Danny. Danny was the bar's only regular, and except for the three bodies at the bar, the cantina was empty.

"Sounds good, I'll join you, there might be a toast or two in keeping with Francisco's bartending tradition. Are you staying over or just stopping to pick up

Alejandro's luggage?" Luc was tempted to bring out the tequila.

"Thought we would, for a couple days anyway. Unless, the spare bedroom you mentioned is occupied."

"Open and ready for visitors." Luc addressed Alejandro.

"Are you stopping in the Barrio to visit your family before heading back?"

"Not in the cards. The Barrio is Lee's Arkansas, a place where gays are taboo. Thanks to the influence of the Catholic church, re-enforced by the macho Mexican thing."

"Analogous to the attitude of the Southern shitkicker."

"Sort of Danny, but it's more a religious-cultural thing than just hate for someone different. What I love about moving to California with Lee is nobody cares what your sexual preferences are, as long as you're having fun."

Luc was off work on Sundays now, Francisco told his wife he needed to pick up the shift to give Luc more study time. The little white lie went a long way in freeing him up from the familia obligations he went to great lengths to avoid. The love birds were only staying through the weekend before heading to their home in California so it was an early night all around. They set sail right after Luc was off to his Monday morning classes. Lee left an open invitation for Luc to come to California after he graduates. Post-graduation was something Luc had not speculated on, he would wait to see which way the wind blows.

Francisco's Sunday escape from the familia did not last long. His esposa gave him an option; if Luc couldn't work on Sunday, close the bar. It was not an option for Francisco as long as Luc was available, his oldest son Hector, in his last throes of undergraduate studies, was not ready to take over the reins. Working Friday afternoon through Sunday evening in a way was a blessing for Luc giving him down time in a quiet bar to hit the books. This became a necessity when once shy Danny invited his classmates Sallie, Miranda, and Caledonia, to first study evenings at the Brew House, followed by the weekends, which quickly turned into party time. It was an arrangement which at first didn't interfere with Luc's sedentary living until Angel scored a shitload of cocaine, and wild and crazy became a daily temptation.

La Cantina soon became the hangout for the girls on weekends eliminating any down time for Luc to study. Danny convinced Francisco to install a jukebox with an eclectic mix of western, conjunto norteño, disco, and rock. This in turn brought in more student nurses, their boyfriends and girlfriends, and increased Francisco's profits along with Luc's workload. It was a long way from Steve White's Wednesday night poetry readings. Like Zippers Danny helped out at the La Cantina pro bono. It was a way to temper the mental temptation which conflicted with the physical and psychological erectile dysfunction caused by his war wound. Both of which were under attack by Caledonia and Miranda. As potential nurses they took on an afterschool project to get a rise out of Danny. Caledonia was not a common Mexican name but one she was labeled with by the Scottish GI from Fort Bliss who impregnated her mother before running off to die in Nam. To add to Danny's excitement they were lesbians, not averse to having fun with boys. One boy in particular, and cocaine was the cherry in the cock-tail.

Roll a dollar bill tight, cut a couple lines with a Silver Astor stainless steel razor blade, and snort. Ignore the nosebleeds, runny nose, difficulty swallowing, and shake and rattle your head as the euphoric feeling stimulates the brain. Coke, snow, or blow, whatever it's called intensifies touch, sound, and sight. Coke it turns out was an aphrodisiac, and Danny and the girls enjoyed every minute of it, even if for him it was a spectator sport most of the time. For Luc on the other hand, the increase in pleasure and stamina from a line or two of coke meant Sallie was not a wallflower in the ever increasing bacchanalia occupying any and all of his extracurricular activity. There was no way he could get Sallie to slow down, and no way, he wanted to; she was nonstop acceleration, and sex was her Disney World. For Luc it had been a dry year even for a desert rat, and whenever Sallie knocked, the door was open. The musician Wilson Picket warned in his song about Mustang Sally 'that he'd put her flat feet on the ground,' with Nurse Sallie, Luc could only go along for the ride never with touching ground.

March break was not a break from the wild and crazy; a Dallas trip to catch Led Zeppelin, memorable for what they could remember of it; hot sauna parties in Juarez, non-stop blow, weed, and booze, left the boys and girls exhausted, and scrambling to finish their mid-terms. For Luc, Danny, and Sallie, all scheduled to graduate, it was smooth sailing through the end of the school year as most classes were secondary to completing projects and papers. Final exams would simply be a re-affirmation of their grade point averages. Luc, didn't take things for granted and managed to hideaway in the library and study. Miranda and Caledonia were both juniors with no intention of curbing their libertine life style. All three ladies decided to abandon the dorm they were staying in, and temporarily move into the Brew House. For Danny, finals were not a problem, he had an in-house study group 24-7.

TWENTY-SIX

Luc hadn't checked his on campus mail box since the last time the Eagle shit. No one was sending him letters, no one knew his address. When he picked up May's final installment on the GI Bill, he found a letter with no return name or address. It was postmarked April 1st, and could have been in his box since the beginning of the month. Inside was a divorce notification from Wyoming, Department of Family Services announcing he was no longer married to Colette. He somehow missed the wedding until he recalled from past experience a common law marriage in Texas simply required setting up a joint bank account, which in a weak moment he did, and Colette most likely told her biker friends at Rosa's Cantina she was hitched. It was a little detail that had the same legal effect as going before a Justice of the Peace. For ease of filing, low filing fee, and minimal processing time, Biker friendly Wyoming was the place to get a divorce. Strike Two. Luc racked up two marriages and possibly two divorces without having done his time. He still wasn't sure his marriage to Allison in Alpine was finalized, which of course would have made him a bigamist on top of everything else.

After a three day blowout the graduation binge
ended in a hangover even Jaime Hut's menudo couldn't
cure. As the lone survivor in the house, Luc surveyed the
damage. The Brew House was a disaster; it was roach city,
the smell of stale beer and cairns of cigarette butts piled in
crusted ashtrays permeated the air, and a culinary
smorgasbord of leftover botanas blanketed the tables and
the counters. The aggravating drone of the swamp cooler
mitigated the vacuous silence. Not only was the party over,
there was no one left to notice. School was out. The
revelers scattered to the four winds. Even Danny, with
Nurse Sallie his new co-pilot, had run off in the van. It
seems there was a bonding in the study group Luc missed.
Danny and Sallie, decided, before coming down off hits of
Orange Sunshine acid, they could double their pleasure, and
headed for Cloudcroft in the New Mexico mountains for
some spiritual enlightenment.

They left a short note on the fridge. A quote from
Steppenwolf's "Born to Be Wild."

get your motor runnin',
head out on the highway,
lookin' for adventure,
and whatever comes our way
Sallie/Danny

Unlike Colette, Danny didn't run off on a hawg, and
he left Luc some of the drugs. The drugs helped to
overcome the lack of motivation to deal with the external
mess he was left with. They did little to relieve the
depression of not having anywhere to turn to, somewhere or
something he could take hold of and follow, to whatever
end. He had finally reached the top of the mountain only to
find there was no way to go but down. He was on the road
again going nowhere, with no destination other than what
tomorrow might bring. He ventured out of the Brew House

only to hang out or work his shifts at La Cantina. With the university on summer slowdown the Cantina catered to locals, mostly Mexicans, and the jukebox played nothing but polka and waltz rhythms of conjunto norteño Bandas. They were story songs of the Mexican working class, Luc knew none of the words, and the beat sounded the same for every song. Somehow he could relate to the sadness and the hope they portrayed in the voices of the singers.

Staying stoned was not a problem. Angel stopped in on his rounds. He could provide updates on Albert and Angelica, and even on occasion fill Luc in on the machinations of Danny and Sallie in Cloud Croft. His customer base reached well into New Mexico. Reading was Luc's sole entertainment, and the only stimulus besides drugs that kept him from running away from himself and his surroundings. He could lose himself in a book. Going somewhere was never going to be enough when the destination is a dead end. Buried in the Brew House his mind ran through scenarios and bounced off possibilities, a pin ball bouncing of bumpers and flippers on its way to a dark hole devoid of answers. He had run from the unknown, searching for an intangible concept of home as long as he could remember. Until now, moving on was always an option of last resort, and carried with it the loneliness and uncertainty he knew too well. By the end of June he reached a point of hopelessness; an inability to make decisions and focus, prevented him from seeing how things could ever get better let alone identifying what he could do to improve his situation, and any amount of help from Angel, he knew would not provide a solution to his dilemma. He was broken down on the side of the road, white trash with nowhere to go.

During the weekday when not working he staked out a table at La Cantina. It was his reading post where he could escape the solitary confinement of the Brew House for the anonymity of a bar. Tequila induced sleep and marijuana anaesthetized the day. It was a Monday evening, the temperature lingered over a hundred degrees for the last two weeks and no sign of relief. Cooking eggs on the sidewalk in El Paso was not a myth. The Brew House, even with the swamp cooler dropping the temperature a few degrees it was the time of year one couldn't escape the heat. Mercifully in La Cantina there was a floor fan and a couple of lumbering overhead fans. Luc, sitting at the bar was the only patron since the lunch time rush hour of two city workers on a liquid cold beer diet came and went. Luc was nursing Sauza, Francisco shared a salutatory shot.

"Tell me Francisco, when you and your family lived in the village of Boquillas, with one light bulb, one cantina, and a shitload of chickens did you ever think about why you were there, and where you were going."

Francisco thought for a minute. He seldom looked back.

"We were too busy with the daily grind to even think about mañanas. Day dreaming as you gringos call it was a luxury we could not afford. Mi padre owned two mules, that proudly could carry a great load of Candelaria. It was on the backs of those mules he was able to save enough to bring us across the river to a new life. Mi padre's load was to carry us through to a better life. Even today I don't think about mañana, for God has blessed me with a means to carry my load." He paused. He was not one to judge another. "What load do you carry Luc?"

"Whatever it is I don't think it's enough to get me across the river to a better life. I guess I've just been going along for the ride. What did you go to university for Francisco, you don't need a four year degree to bartend?"

"I went not to graduate with a letter after my name, only to gain the skills to help me carry my load, to help my familia: how to speak English, how to run a business, how to survive in a gringo world."

"It obviously worked for you. Salud!"

135

"And you amigo. You tell me it took you a long, long time to get those letters, now what do you do with them? Can they buy you a couple mules?"

Luc spent all those years chasing after something which in the end turned out to be never enough. The pot at the end of the rainbow was just a pot, and not even a pot to piss in.

"I got the letters, but I can't see any use for them now that I have them. I don't feel any wiser than when I got out of the Army. At least that gave me life experience. Since I was discharged there have been some good times, mostly though, life has been nothing but an experience down one dead end after another."

"I saw you reading 100 Years of Solitude, you know Gabriel García Márquez. He once wrote "*la sabiduría nos llega cuando ya no nos sirve de nada*," wisdom comes to us when it's already too late. You are young Luc, it's not too late for you to find what you're looking for. Not too late to find the answers to why you are here, and where you are going."

At one time Luc thought approaching thirty was old, over the hill, and yet he hadn't even begun to carry a load. He had followed Rilke's advice in *Letters to a Young Poet*, the only way out of living on the down side is to make the most of it and move on.

"I hear you Francisco, I know it's never too late, it's just my mañana is a blank slate right now. Since I was a kid, when the shit hit the fan I thought it was my fault, my problem to solve, and by running away from it, hiding from it, pretending it didn't happen it would all go away. Whatever the problem it got better because I could bury the fault deep inside of me, and it went away in time. Time was the cure all, as was moving on."

"*Hay más tiempo que vida,* there's more time than life. You have not stopped moving on."

"You're right about that Francisco, I also became adept at being invisible, shrinking when I would face dominance, then seeking out hiding places, like a cat's penchant for cubby holes and boxes. I had my cubby holes and boxes to hide in and feel safe. The things people remember about their childhood should be all the joyful happenings; I carry with me playing alone in a back yard, people I'd come to trust leaving and not returning."

"And getting stoned and drinking has now become your safe place, maybe?"

"I see wisdom does come with age. Salud! Tell me how many saludos are in a bottle of Tequila?"

"This is where my business courses at the university came in handy." He held the half empty bottle of Sauza up. "It generally takes at least two people to raise a salute, and I have calculated twenty-five shots at twenty-nine milliliters in a 750 milliliter bottle divided by two would be twelve a piece, and we fight over the last one."

"You certainly got more capital out of your courses than I did in the English Department."

"Luc, you always have a book with you and I see you reading all the time. Maybe you find something in the pages to help you see what you don't know you are looking for. You need to find *tu pasión*."

Finding Hemingway

TWENTY-SEVEN

Luc reckoned his wallet size laminated diploma must be worth something when it came to landing fulltime employment. He needed a decent job to pay the rent, cover utilities, and help maintain the vehicle Francisco had given him rent to buy with the money he was earning part-time at La Cantina. It was a fix or repair driveway 1959 Volkswagen microbus, his esposa had been praying for him to get rid of for years. Beyond those necessities anything he could earn was gravy. Savings, life insurance, retirement planning were ghosts of a future yet to come. Unlike many previous adventures he now had a résumé, what he still lacked was a career goal, and as Francisco so deftly pointed out, he needed, a passion for something. Passion is like fuel for the car, without it he was stuck on a highway going nowhere.

Luc picked up an El Paso Herald Post and scanned the help wanted ads, a skill he had honed outside of university. Sales was out; being a non-consumer it would be hard for him to convince someone to buy something. Legal was out; he had made every effort in life to avoid getting involved in anything legal, except of course matrimony. Financial, management, marketing, and medical, all required him to spend another ten years chasing the alphabet: BS, BFA, BBA etc. Construction, too hot,

Restaurants, too busy—nothing appealed to him, nor did he think he could qualify for any of them. Living in a city, eighty percent Hispanic, the language of labor was Spanish and he lacked the language gene except for French. No French listed in the ads as a necessary skill. Under retail he finally found a posting somewhat interesting—Used Books, customer service, full time, apply within. It gave a downtown Stanton Street address. Actually right around the block from La Cantina. His courses in the English Department provided him with a competent literary background. As for a marketable retail skill, that was dubious territory, at best his BA prepared him for collecting honey buckets in Alaska. He considered himself well read with, as Francisco pointed out, a pasión for books, A used bookstore seemed a reasonable step into the world of working for the man.

"Don't worry about the salary, I just need enough to live on, pay the rent and occasionally eat. I'm mainly after the experience."

Luc had practiced the line over and over standing in front of a mirror. It sounded right although he didn't have a clue whether it made a hill of beans to the stern face in front of him, reminding him of a drill Sargent in boot camp who scared the shit out of him. Unlike previous interviews there was nothing standing out surrounding the interviewer Luc could connect him to, except thousands of books. The Colonel, stood at attention behind the front counter reviewing Luc's creative résumé. He read over the one page document, periodically looking up at the potential recruit who, in stark contrast to the military demeanor of a retired army officer sported a Jesus haircut, wore a peasant shirt, faded Levis, and Viet Cong combat boots. Luc regretted his decision to wear sandals instead of his Justins.

The Colonel's brush cut was compromised by a few balding spots, and at the tips of his pyramidal moustache there was a hint of a twist. His height was exaggerated by a rigid spine. A barrage of eyebrows were eves troughs above round eyeglasses balanced on the tip his nose, and Luc noted the type John Lennon wore. With the exception of his sloping shoulders, and a slight belly over the belt, revealing years behind a desk, he was the personification of a retired Full Bird Colonel. The Colonel knew a good bet when he saw it; cheap labor, and a young Vet to boot. Luc was ex-Army, the Colonel was Army to the core, who suffered the lesser of the ranks. He was not given to small talk, chatter or casual rumination, except when it came to his beloved books. He hired Luc on the spot. Another curious pattern in his life a repeat performance of his time in Dallas.

"Thirty-five hours a week, Tuesday through Saturday, 10 sharp, here until 5, or when the last customer leaves, minimum starting wage, and you start tomorrow morning. That work for you?"

Luc didn't hesitate or care what the job description was going to be, and he wasn't in any position to negotiate. "Works for me. Sir."

The Colonel placed the résumé on top of a pile of paper in a basket on the desk.

"Let's see if we can make a bookman out of you Corporal. Look around if you want to. By the way, what's the last book you've read?"

Luc was quick to respond. *"Been Down So Long It Looks Like Up to Me,"* by Richard Fariña. It's the adventures of Gnossos Pappadopoulis, similar to Odysseus. Luc couldn't tell whether the expression on the Colonel's face was one of approval or distain. After he was dismissed, he spent over an hour perusing the stacks. On leaving the bookstore, the Colonel was still standing at the front desk shuffling papers.

"10 o'clock sharp." He didn't look up.

Minimum wage was two dollars and ten cents, amounting to seventy-three bucks a week, before taxes, covering the basics, and then some. If a roommate came along to split the rent he'd be laughing. On the outside chance the microbus bit the dust, he was a block away from the bus stop on Piedras Street, and a direct line downtown to the bookstore, and La Cantina. If Luc had the image of working in a bookstore as being a genteel occupation it was short lived. He soon discovered the basic business of books was all about hauling cartons from one spot to another, fending off the onslaught of dust compliments of a desert environment, and the never ending process of shelving, pricing, and cataloguing. The Colonel estimated he had accumulated over twenty thousand volumes in a warehouse space located in the rear of the store, and half that amount or more on the retail shelves. His command center was on an open platform above the warehouse. From there he had a commanding view over the long narrow aisles lined with bookshelves leading to the front of the store. No one climbed the wrought iron staircase to the Full Bird's nest unless there was a deal in the making from book buyers and collectors.

In the warehouse books were piled on the floor, overflowed carton upon carton, and were crammed into precariously leaning bookcases that towered to the edge of unshaded light bulbs. It was home for collections and fragments of Baum, Conrad, Burton, Burroughs, Twain, and Faulkner, among a legion of other authors. National Geographics from year one huddled next to air-brushed nipples and bare ankles of early Playboys. At first Luc could find no rhyme or reason to what was stored in the back rooms. The Colonel was a horder of authors, and there was little excess room in the front stacks where Huckleberry Finn and the Arabian Nights went cover to cover with Gothic Romances and Pulps. It was truly an asylum of words, a gold mine for the bibliomaniac.

The Colonel had not mentioned a word about being a mentor, Luc however felt he was beginning his apprenticeship starting on the selling floor, and the warehouse would come later. His task was to separate unlikely companions, relocate lost souls, and market their spines and covers to the world, and something no one previously put the time and effort into—label, label, label. It was all grunt work at first, but it also gave Luc a feel for the place. He discovered the Colonel's uncanny ability to know where any book was, in the warehouse, or on the shelves. It was a skill for Luc to strive for.

"We'll get to the good stuff later," the Colonel advised Luc one day, "after you've worked in the trenches for a spell." What you might consider confusion, this 'worship of writers', is simply unemployment of order in a congress of chaos." The Colonel loved to phrase his words in venereal terms when speaking of his empire of books. "I want you to find the order Corporal. It's called merchandising, and it's one of the keys to selling books."

The Colonel was a recognized collector and expert on Southwest Literature with the works of Wally McRae— cowboy, poet and philosopher, revered authors Owen Wister, Louis L'Amour, Max Brand, and in a special place, on his private shelves, the first edition of Theodore Roosevelt's *Winning the West*; an aficionado of Bullfighting his collection included prize first editions of Hemingway's *The Dangerous Summer*, *Fiesta,* and *Death in the Afternoon* alongside Tom Lea's *Bullfight Manual for Spectators*, and dozens more, on display in dust free bookshelves in his chamber, along with the oeuvre of his favorite author, Hemingway. He eventually invited Luc to climb the stairs, and allowed him to browse through those sacrosanct collections at his leisure. At times he would get out from behind his large oak desk, and with a slight hint of tenderness, pick out a book, holding it momentarily in his stubby hands as if it were made out of porcelain, and hand it to Luc, followed by a disquisition on its value, both content and physical condition. It was not until Luc held in his own hands a first edition of Hemingway's 1927 *Men*

Without Women, a rare collection of early short stories, he truly began to realize there was more to being a bookman than sorting and labeling.

"A good book is like a fine brown skinned woman, made for the hand, the eye, and capable of overwhelming the mind. *Take Death in the Afternoon*," he removed the book from the bookcase, this is a first edition, 1932, signed by the author. The copy is Fine, illustrated with a front piece by Juan Gris, and on the front cover the upper board stamped with the author's name in gilt, in Hemingway's own script. If, or when you finally become a bookman Corporal you will be able to recognize a book's condition and value, and describe it front to back."

The Colonel's fingers working the book somehow reminded Luc of a blind man reading braille. He put the book back on the shelf, lining the spine perfectly with the other volumes, stepped back sharply, and checking the alignment as if they were soldiers standing at attention waiting for inspection. It was these occasions that made the Colonel's remoteness an acceptable byproduct of being right where Luc wanted to be. This he assumed was what Francesco meant by finding your passion. When he first walked under the three bells chiming over the entrance he knew *As New* and he knew *Poor,* referencing a book's condition, now he was on his way to learning everything in-between.

At first few days went by without the Colonel coming down for a short stroll among the stacks while Luc trailed behind him. One area of interest that brought him out of his chambers was checking on the progress Luc made on organizing and labelling the genres. Even without the labels there was a modicum of order enabling people with patience and time to find something of interest. Cookbooks, children's books, Art, dictionaries, and travel were pretty evident without labels. Religion, health, science, math, history, and biographies—somewhat self-evident, but when it came to fiction: mystery, sci-fi, romance, drama, classic literature, action and adventure, they were all alphabetized by the authors last name, at least by the first letter of the last name, and all required separation by sub-types and individual identification—fantasy next to sci-fi, Harlequin next to Romance.

Luc needed a pen and pad when the Colonel wanted to talk about book descriptors. He'd pull books off the shelves and work them as if he were kneading dough; this one New, in the same condition when it was first published, another one Fine or Very Good, with no defects or little signs of wear. Those were few and far between in a used bookstore. On average most were Good or Fair, previously loved with signs they were worn by handling, chipped, damp-stained, sunned, shaken or showing shelf wear from just sitting around waiting to be read. Nothing below the level of Fair ever reached a bookshelf in the Colonels store, he simply would not buy Poor, and if it came in under the bells, he'd toss it.

Luc gave up expecting the Colonel to call him by his name, it was always Corporal, as if he were some kind of time warp. Matter of fact Luc couldn't recall addressing the Colonel by his real name, which he only learned reading the incoming mail he would deliver daily to his chamber—Ewan Balfour Scott. Being Scottish Luc surmised, might have had something to do with his views on selling books. His motto was buy for a dime and sell for a dollar. In contradiction to his profit motivation Luc knew he would overprice a book if he felt it had value as a collector's item, on the other hand he'd sell a book for a nickel if he wasn't enamored with the author or content. Waiting on demand for the books he priced high in the El Paso walk-in market turned out to be waiting for Godot, and possibly why the Colonel had a plethora of volumes stacked up in the warehouse. There was a huge disparity between book retailing and book collecting, and Luc came to realize the real money was in capitalizing on collectors, and knowing what books dealers worldwide were looking for. Books achieve a degree of rarity only when demand exceeds supply, which keeps the bookman forever chasing demand, and this, it turned out, was the market keeping the Colonel in business.

It was late August when the Colonel descended from his chambers and approached Luc at the check-out counter.

"Corporal I think you are beginning to get the hang of this book business."

He was light on compliments, this was a big one. Luc made the mistake of suggesting maybe they should focus on promoting and selling books. He had come to the conclusion merchandising and advertising were the keys to the retail kingdom. Before he could retract the statement the Colonel had his arm wrapped around his shoulder and was dragging him down the aisles.

"Sell books you say!"

There was a ragged edge to his normally sharp tone, similar to a drill sergeant honing in for the kill.

"This is not a supermarket Corporal. Not the shopping mall outlet where they stack and rotate books like cans of peas and carrots. This is a bookstore."

Keeping Luc in an arm lock he ran his free hand across a row of 19th century classics: Anna Karenina, Moby Dick, Crime and Punishment, Great Expectations, which the Colonel noted, Luc labeled correctly.

"Here you have an unrelenting portrait of mankind's vices and weaknesses: adultery, obsession, madness, vanity, suffering, vengeance, and redemption." He turned down the next aisle. "On these shelves are 'a brow of scholars,' 'a wrangle of philosophers,' real people, each with a little something to say. Some a little less than others I admit, but all of them are muttering something about the human condition. We are in the business of transferring knowledge, and any profit we make in doing that is simply paying the bills."

The Colonel halted at the end of the aisle where Luc had labeled several rows of Gothic romances and Harlequins.

"Now this," He swung Luc around to face the shelves, his arm still wrapped securely around his shoulders in a totally out of character display of what could be construed as familiarity, "this you sell for its historical value. In between the sheets of this soft pornography, sprinkled with a little bondage there is a semblance of history—it's what you sell. Each of these books contains some germ of intelligence that kept the author up all night typing while the readers of the world slept and waited."

He marched Luc past the Science Fiction, Fantasy, and Occult, randomly dusting the spines with his finger, until they reached the front of the store. Luc slipped out of the Colonel's grasp and stood by the check-out counter. The Colonel turned to stare out the window at the passing traffic. His building was just off the beaten track, and since he carried few books in Spanish, with the majority of downtown El Paso pedestrians were Mexican, he didn't have much of a walk-in trade.

"It's what we are here for Corporal, to transfer knowledge." His voice lost the edge, as he continued to scan the street. "There isn't anything we need to know that's not in some book, somewhere, and if we make a little profit in disseminating knowledge, well, it's just good business…at least, that's the way it's supposed to work."

The Colonel did an about face, and before Luc could offer a couple suggestions on how they might promote dissemination, he quick-timed it back to his chambers. Soft porn with a little bondage, for Luc this was a rare look at the Colonel's humorous side.

He had no idea where the path he was on would lead. The Colonel was a wealth of information, and Luc felt he was learning a great deal from him about the practical and esoteric knowledge of what it takes to be a bibliophile, beyond just the love of books. Other than working weekends at La Cantina over the summer, Luc's life slowed to escaping in the evenings with a good book. Cocaine was not an option for fear of sliding down the rabbit hole again. His drug consumption narrowed to the occasional doobie. He gave up thinking about a roommate, and became for the first time in a long time, comfortable with himself. He was no longer chasing rainbows looking for a pot of gold... until.

TWENTY-EIGHT

His eyesore had been very reliable in spite of the fact Luc knew nothing about the maintenance of vehicles, especially when it came to keeping them running. In reminiscence of his first go with a White Trash he left on the side of the road in Arkansas, the Volkswagen needed tender loving care, and now with a means to an end he parked it with a local mechanic for rest and restoration, and took the bus. It was not a problem in El Paso, buses being the main transportation for the Hispanic population. Getting to and fro the bookstore was no problem, La Cantina on weekend shifts was another issue. Caledonia and Miranda still hung out at La Cantina on most weekends, and they often gave Luc a ride home. Often enough to take interest in cutting out of the dorm, a drag on their lesbian social life, and taking up residency at the brew house with Luc. How it all came together in a short space he didn't know, he just knew his life had unexpectedly moved from neutral into second gear.

Luc's immersion in the business of books went well beyond merchandizing and marketing, and the Colonel, a consummate bibliophile lived by one of his favorite quotes by Henry Miller, "A book lying idle on a shelf is wasted ammunition." The Colonel had his own special way of dealing with customers. Collectors, especially those after Texas, Southwestern, and Mexicana genres knew the Colonel had them all, and there was a bottle of Johnnie Walker, and topical conversation waiting in the Colonel's chamber. Dealers were first on the food chain; and the dealers held free reign in the warehouse. Outside of observing their coming and goings, Luc had little contact with most of them. Then there were the regulars, the steady customers who had, he assumed by their laser focus, been coming to the bookstore since it opened. They could spend hours roaming the stacks, absorbed in their own worlds. The Colonel would occasionally come down from his chambers to indulge in a little reminiscence, and maybe offer a suggestion on a read. The few and far between casual walk-ins were Luc's domain. The Colonel's claim they were the lifeblood of the business, didn't jive with the cash register receipts.

"You have to cater to all kinds," he said during one of his lessons, "a customer walks into a shoe store barefoot and right away you know what he's after; all you need is size, style, and price. With books, you can't tell by looking at a customer whether they are interested in rock art, orangutans or the philosophy of science. The secret of selling books is to know how to entice a person into talking about what they are interested in, what their passion is. To quote Christopher Morley, 'When you sell a man a book you don't sell him just twelve ounces of paper and ink and glue—you sell him a whole new life.' Everybody is an expert on something and they love to talk about it. A bookman listens. And it's imperative to know what you have on the shelves when they identify what they are interested in. Remember that, and you might sell a book or two."

WHEN SOMEWHERE IS NEVER ENOUGH

It was a lesson Luc worked hard to master, especially when it came to customers like Oru Banner. He came into the store once a week wearing the same blue faded double breasted suit of a kind that goes in and out of style for decades. He hid any acknowledgement of Luc underneath a sweat stained International Harvester baseball cap, and on the rare occasion he found a book to buy it was a silent transaction at the checkout counter. The Colonel said he was a walking encyclopedia of the years 1895 thru 1900. How he knew this was a mystery for Luc who never actually saw them acknowledge each other's existence. In a one-time attempt to break the ice, Luc proffered a volume published in 1900: *The History of Negro Soldiers in the Spanish-American War, and Other Items of Interest*, written by Edward A. Johnson. Oru's silent response underneath his cap beak made Luc feel he was prying into his private sex life.

Luc savored a conversation with anyone wanting to dialogue about authors and content, for almost every customer has their unique blend of genre, era, and reading level, and there was plenty of time to listen. With deference to the rotating whackos, his goal was to have anyone who entered the Colonel's bookstore leave with a volume cradled in their hand. Frank and Bob were unique in the scheme of things. Frank was a frequent buyer, and his choice of paperback books eclectic. Bob, an ex-marine nurse, and as Luc discovered Frank's caregiver, only hung out at the front desk and avoided venturing into the stacks. The singular topic he talked about was horseracing. Frank was a disheveled six foot stuffed teddy bear with coke bottle glasses, a permanent five o'clock shadow under a tangle of uncombed hair. Frank was always smiling, and because he was supposedly mute, conversation about the content of a book was out of the question. He did however have an eye for covers, and Luc was always able to comment on his choice, and expand it to a tidbit or two about the content. Charles Dickens wrote "there are books of which the backs and covers are by far the best parts," and Frank's choice of covers, however, generally held content worth reading.

Selling was just part of the learning process, and except for the paperbacks, which were already dirt cheap, all prices were negotiable. Searching for and purchasing stock at the cheapest price possible was one of the more challenging and profitable aspects of the book business; walk-ins and classifieds being the two main sources. On weekends the Colonel would hone in on potential sites in the daily press; church bazars, estate sales, and yard sales. At first the Colonel led the way, setting out at the crack of dawn to be in the front of the line, Luc would tag behind pro bono, and half asleep. When he found a gem, he'd play it like winning a hand of poker, never letting the person know what he held in his hand, and playing the role of discourager at the quality of what he was begrudgingly willing to pay for. He had a way of making the seller feel like he was the recipient of the Colonels generosity for taking the books off their hands. Scouring for books was like panning for gold, plenty of cold water runs through your hands before you find a nugget. The Colonel found a first edition Hemmingway in an attic, paid a quarter and sold it for fifteen hundred. He had an endless number of similar stories. There was a simple formula for pricing an attic full, box, or an armful of books. He would estimate the return on investment of one or two items, and it would be his bottom line for the lot. Gradually the Colonel backed off of the early morning chase and left it all to Luc. Luc felt turning the hunt over to him wasn't so much confidence in his ability, for he rarely came down from his chambers anymore when someone came in with a bag or box of books to sell or trade, the Colonel seemed to be losing interest. Buying and pricing books were the latest stripes Luc earned and the hazards of mold and mildew came with the lesson. One day Luc held in his hand a near perfect book, except for a pervasive dank smell, and asked the Colonel if there was any way to get rid of the odor. The Colonel took the book, flipped the pages, and ran it by his nose.

"Toss it. You don't want it in the store. It's got mold on it. The smell is caused by mildew. Molds digest paper and book bindings. It spreads like a virus to other books, you don't want it on the shelf. It's something a bookman has to live with. Oh yes, and once you get those spores up your nose you'll forever recognize the smell in any book."

This was the sort of lesson Luc wished he'd received before crawling through dank attics and basements, and spending months nose to nose with hundreds of used books. Luc was at the front desk sorting through a newly acquired box of books, stacking them in two piles; one to be donated to the Salvation Army—heaven for book club editions, binding copies where covers are shot, and any with musty odors—and the other pile for resale. When the Colonel approached the counter he was gently cradling in his hands an old volume long since buried in the warehouse. Luc was in for a Colonel moment.

"Corporal, look at how this design is raised on the cover, they just don't bother putting this much work into a book anymore."

He was holding a beautifully hand-tooled leather bound copy of Sir Walter Scott's Lady of the Lake, published in 1810.

"The engravings still contained tissue-guard, it has the foxing we've talked about, brown spotting caused by chemical reaction in a book of this age, there's some shelf wear, and look," he turned the book in his hands, "the binding is solid and tight...used to be bookbinders were artists."

Luc sensed the same note of sadness in his voice as when he talked about the dying breed of soldier, or the vanishing cowboy.

"Now they just cut and glue, cut and glue." He pointed out a couple small holes on the back cover. "Look at this, clean through. It's what a book worm will do, it's called worming. Drill a hole clean as a needle through butter. Leave a book on a wooden shelf too long and the larvae of the death watch beetle will tunnel right through the heart of it."

He stood staring at the needle holes for a few minutes. "Mark Twain would have tossed it into the Mississippi and fed those worms to the fish, that's what he thought of Scott." Luc caught the Lady in midair as the Colonel abruptly turned on his heels and marched back to his chambers, dismissing her completely.

At first Luc was taken off guard when the Colonel suggested he stick around after work and commune with the literary ghosts. It was another out of character moment, but it soon became Luc's favorite time of day, the short time it lasted. Twain would be down one aisle reliving his days on the river or berating missionaries, Burton, down another aisle could be heard arguing over the source of the Nile, on another shelf Sweitzer tuning an organ, Zane Grey spinning tales of the West, or Marsh and Cope battling over old bones. On occasion the Colonel would characterize a book by its physical amenities; mostly though, on these perambulations, it was what was in between the pages penned by the authors, composers, painters and bards. In the dim and dusty stacks the air filled with the din of the comic and the cantankerous, the angry and the content, the sinner and the saintly. The Colonel had a way of bringing books to life.

It was the end of September when the Colonel abruptly ended, without explanation the after work salon among the literary intelligentsia; business ground to an occasional paperback, buying books was put on hold until further notice. There was an increase in dealers, and book collectors visiting the Colonel, and wandering around the warehouse ignoring Luc, giving him plenty of time to sit back and read. There was only so much dusting and re-arranging one could do with the books. He brought order into their lives, made them accessible, rescued them from the bottom of boxes, and in due time, somehow they would find a place in someone's library, in someone's heart and mind.

"When you become a bookman," the Colonel told him, "you make the transition yourself, moving from one of the boxes of life into a world where the only limitation is your time to read."

TWENTY-NINE

Luc began to speculate about what the Colonel might be up to as the occasion of dealers dropping into the bookstore increased dramatically. On the first day of October he got up the nerve to confront the Colonel on the obvious—change was happening. He'd been here before. Luc considered himself a pro at just going with the flow. It was not out of concern for he couldn't see any alternative to what he was doing, but curiosity got the best of him. It was closing time. He flipped the sign and locked the door and approached the wrought iron staircase with just a slight hesitation in his footsteps, for he wasn't sure if he wanted to know what was up. When he stood at the entrance to the chamber the Colonel was on the phone and gestured for him to take a seat. His desk was piled with a clutter of paper, a venereal term Luc was sure to the Colonel's liking, however, it was totally unlike him. As if he were expecting an early morning muster and inspection, he was persnickety about keeping his space prim and proper. When he finished his conversation on the phone he swiveled around and faced his prized book collections. Luc followed his gaze noticing a number of holes in the bookcase, and it wasn't worming. Where his prize bullfight collection used to be, there was one book and a half empty bottle of Johnnie Walker Red. The Colonel swiveled facing Luc and leaned back in his chair.

"I suppose you need an explanation Mr. Barbon. I'm sure you noticed something was in the works. I was holding off discussing the pending changes until the powder was dry and I had all my guns loaded."

It was his habit to get right to the point; and it was the first time he call Luc by his given name. Informing the troops before they absolutely needed to know was never an option for the Colonel, it just encouraged opposition.

"Don't worry, your job is safe, just planning on re-inventing ourselves. The book business is just not happening financially. I've carried it for years. Tough to make a go of it in this climate, and I'm not talking about the weather. Oh sure, we're managing, hanging on, but only, and we need to up the ante."

Luc sat silently while the Colonel ran down all the pluses for the changes about to happen—no, that we're in the process of unfolding quickly. As if he were describing the content and condition of a book he continued with his breakdown of the plans in process.

"Over the next week we'll be working on emptying out the warehouse. We already have a number of buyers lined up. Starting soon we'll advertise cut rate prices for what's left on the shelves. It'll be a buyers' market. We'll start stocking the warehouse with our new line as soon as we have room. Once we remove the bookcases we'll start remodeling, with display cases, and clothing racks. Merchandizing comes next and voilà: the 'PEOPLE'S EMPORIUM' will open in time for Halloween."

It was easily over 80 degrees in the Colonel's chamber even with a swamp cooler blowing strong; Luc could feel a chill run up his back at the thought of all those wonderful literary writers stuffed in boxes and hauled away.

"What's an Emporium?" Is all he was able to muster."

"Emporium is a Greek term used to denote a store which sells a wide variety of goods. We are going to carry costumes for sale and for rent, masquerade and theatrical make up, colorful wigs, hairpieces, all sorts of wacky, cool, creepy paraphernalia including books, incense, and candles. We'll be a one stop shopping store for Halloween."

Luc made every effort to maintain a calm demeanor when normally talking to the Colonel, in deference to the master/apprentice role he assumed. Now, behind his stoic mask was a tumultuous litter of incredulity, disbelief, skepticism, and doubt.

"And what about after Halloween?" the words dribbled out of his mouth.

"No problem, we'll be a tourist attraction in El Paso. We'll have all sorts of hard to find party items people will want all year round. I've done my homework on the marketability and demand in the community. Look at how the Mexicans celebrate the Day of the Dead. They don't read books but they love gory stuff."

He stood up and transferred the bottle of scotch and a couple glasses to his desk. Can I offer you a shot? Let's toast to our new adventure."

In any other context Luc would have felt honored to share a drink with the Colonel, a custom reserved for the dealers. He was still trying to connect Dia de la Muerte with Halloween, two completely different worlds, so he thought.

"Yes, thanks." *No Way*, were the dominant words in his mind.

"You'll be playing an important role in the transition, and I can see a need for someone, someday, to manage the day to day. First things first though, the dealers will shortly be coming to get their books, I want you to make sure they're inventoried, boxed and out the door. We'll work on the rest over the next few weeks."

It was evident to Luc the Colonel had this all worked out, and the trick or treats would be coming in while the genres were being shipped out.

"I'm glad we finally got around to having this little talk Mr. Barbon."

He raised his half full glass, Luc raised his half empty one.

"Here's to success!"

The Colonel put his empty glass on the desk, sat down and picked up the phone. The conversation was over with. *Someday*, Luc knew was the operative word. He was dismissed, and as he started to descended into the stacks he saw the Colonel filling his glass, and he knew, deep down, he had to feel the same sadness he was feeling. He could not see himself in "Dr. Ewan's House of Horrors" selling red dye and wax teeth. His apprenticeship came to an abrupt end, that was the reality, and he felt he only just finished the first book in a trilogy and wanted more.

For Luc his apprenticeship was a success, he found his passion, and it gave him direction—Bookman, had a righteous ring to it. How the future would unfold he couldn't yet imagine. On his way to the front of the store he paused at 'a wrangle of philosophers' and touched the spine of Schopenhauer's *Selected Essays*, and remembered a quote he had read by the philosopher: "We take the sting out of life by accepting it as it is." Luc knew the one book the Colonel was still searching for to round of his oeuvre of Hemingway was the 1937 first edition of *To Have and Have Not*. It did not seem likely now he would ever have it. He wrote the Colonel a note and a quote, and left it on the front counter.

Adios Colonel
"you can't get away from yourself
by moving from one place to another."
- The Sun Also Rises.

Gone to finish my apprenticeship,
thanks for the kick start.
Corporal Luc

Luc put his hands over his ears to drown out the Godspeed from a thousand friends he had made, and walked out the door into the sunlight, hearing the three bells knell overhead for the last time.

THIRTY

Someday just never seemed to quite arrive on Luc's doorstep, and when it approached, it was gone as soon as he opened the door. The philosopher's 'acceptance' took the sting out but it left a numbness, a Novocain on the brain. The rollercoaster ride he'd been on forever was a twister with turns, and crossovers, on an unpredictable track, now he hit the bottom of the drop, and he was looking at a straight run hopefully with no turns or curves.

He applied for jobs at Walden's and B. Dalton's chain bookstores in the Mall; both of which were on the basement level, no windows, florescent lights, and required Luc to wear a tie. With no other options he put his bookman apprenticeship on hold, and took on the role of manservant. Caledonia and Miranda were perfect roommates, on a permanent high. They were busy, seniors in the university nursing program, regulars at The Pet Shop, and hosted a steady stream of students escaping the confines of university housing, visiting the Brew House day and night. Luc put his culinary skills to work, and was chief cook and bottle washer. Constantly surrounded by would be nurses who were uno, bi, and tri sexual, he enjoyed a milieu which had its rewards; mentally in putting any worries behind him, and physically with the absence of inhibition in a carnal playhouse. For Luc it was a passion play without the guilt. Danny and Sallie arrived for Thanksgiving armed with two turkeys, and along with two kegs of beer, the backyard rooftop was the perfect spot for two dozen pilgrims. Sallie had called ahead to her sisters, and booked the third bedroom into the New Year. Now that they were a pair, she'd bring Danny along for old time's sake.

With the onslaught of winter Cloudcroft was knee deep in snow, and all but deserted except for the hardy and hunkered down. Danny and Sallie were living in the Lincoln National Forest with Smokey the bear. Cloudcroft, with a scattered population of around 500 souls at the best of time, consisted of a few buildings along Burro Street they called downtown. They had rented a live-in store front, and planned on opening, once a customer could reach them without snowshoes, an alternative health store, an area Sallie was knowledgeable in. With their nursing backgrounds they thought they'd be able to find a niche in a community of hippies and nature lovers. Danny's access to plenty of drugs through Angel, and his hydroponic gardening skills would supplement their income, and provide the local population with a little uplifting during the deep dark winter, and a whole lot more sunshine during the tourist season.

Francisco was glad to have Luc available for the holidays, where in the Barrio it was Mexican fiesta time from the middle of November through the first weeks of January, and he couldn't escape his familia obligations. Along with the weekends Francisco had plenty of work for Luc during the weekdays if he wanted it. Luc didn't have the inner motivation or given his living conditions the energy to scour the help wanted ads, and since he'd paid off the Volkswagen, and the mechanic had added a few years to its life, shared rent covered his expenses. The cost of living in El Paso, compared to the rest of the States was dirt cheap, if you went native. La Cantina quieted down during semester finals, to be followed by an exodus of staff and students from the university. It was maids a milking, five days till Christmas, and for a Saturday night all through the La Cantina not a creature was stirring when Albert dropped in. Luc had not seen him since he had visited the bookstore with Angelica.

Luc was sitting at a table reading Lowry's *Under the Volcano* when Albert pulled up a chair.

"An alcoholic Brit in Quauhnahuac, on Día de los Muertos, is a long way from *How the Grinch Stole Christmas*."

"I needed something to cheer me up, it seems all the festivities are happening elsewhere. How's it going Albert?"

Albert was noticeably not wearing a tie, and he sported a seasonal red cardigan.

"Couldn't be better. I don't see a bartender, should I help myself to a shot of the gasoline you sell?"

"I'll get it. I need the exercise." Luc returned with a bottle of Sauza and two glasses, and sat down. "How's married life in the Barrio?"

"Angelica's pregnancy is coming to term, and she's in great shape. I'm on my way to being a family man. I'm becoming totally integrated into the Hispanic community. The Barrio is alive."

"Salud! I suspect it's all about votes for their up and coming future councilman." Luc was not being sarcastic. "So, what brings you out bar hopping on the weekend before happy holidays?"

"I'm on a mission. By the way I hear Danny and his girlfriend are back in town. Thought I might see them here."

"They're supposed to be staying behind door number three at the Brew House, I hardly ever see them, accept when they surface for food." Luc filled the glasses. "You're on a mission? Anything to do with Papá Noel."

"I've been asked if I knew anyone who might be interested in a certain proposition, and I thought of you. One of the attributes of a politician is racking up favors for those who can contribute to one's election. Don't know anyone who loves books the way you do, and when I heard you quit the bookstore downtown what they're looking for just might be a fit."

"I didn't actually quit, the bookstore quit me. It's a long story. I'm open to whatever, as long as it's more exciting than this." He gestured toward the empty bar. "What's the gig?"

"This person has a son, who it seems opening a bookstore is his only goal in life, and they need someone, not just anyone, to manage it."

"Isn't that someone they should advertise for in the Herald?"

"Not exactly, there are some complications. Do you remember two guys who I'm told frequented your bookstore? Frank and Bob are their names. Bob's a psychiatric nurse, or something of that ilk, and Frank has some disorder requiring a caregiver. I didn't go into it with my contact, just her son isn't capable of running it himself and needs a proxy. I guess this guy Frank can't talk, or doesn't talk, mute maybe, I don't know. He did graduate from UTEP. Bob has been with him all through university and is his constant companion."

"I remember those two. One of them, Frank I guess, would spend hours in the stacks, and pick out one book to take with him. The bald guy hung around the front desk and rattled on about horse racing at Sunland Park. Told me Frank looks for a cover he takes a liking to when he buys a book. I thought most of Frank's choices were excellent reading myself. Found them both a little strange. Harmless though. By proxy do you mean run the store?"

"There is no store, but yes, my contact wants both a mentor for Frank, and someone who can make the bookstore a reality from scratch."

"It'd be worth checking out, I got nothing to lose. How does this contact, I think you said she, envision this happening? Is there a reason why she doesn't have a name?"

"If interested she wants you to meet with her son Frank, and Bob. Bob McQueen would be your go to guy. The reason I can't mention her name is also complicated. If you take on the project I'll fill you in on what I know."

"I'm game." Luc didn't have to think about it, anything to shake off the dust.

"Salud! He put his empty glass on the table. "Wish you'd upgrade on the tequila."

"When do I meet up with this FranknBob?" Luc topped up the glasses.

"Saturday the 29th, 1 o'clock at the Plaza Hotel. They'll be waiting at a table in the restaurant."

Albert filled him in on his new life. He was busy working on his Masters, learning Spanish, and hanging out at the Mayor's office. Won't run for local office until he graduates. Angelica's family opened all the doors to the Hispanic community. His real goal is the State legislature. Luc didn't have much to add to the conversation. He wondered what Albert's life would be like right now if he and Kate had stayed together; for that matter, what his life would have turned out if she stayed with him. He was happy for Albert, and upon reflection, 'what might have been' didn't carry a helluva lot of Christmas cheer with it.

THIRTY-ONE

Entering the lobby of the Plaza Hotel brought back a wave of memories, all good. It was four years ago, almost to the day Pam booked a suite to stay in while he registered for university and she searched for an apartment. It was all ancient history considering what transpired since. His eyes adjusted slowly as he stepped out of the bright afternoon light into the dimly lit windowless Art-Deco style restaurant. Frank and Bob were the only patrons in the place, sitting at the back of the room at a table lit by banker lights with green alabaster glass shades reminding him of Campisi's Egyptian Restaurant in Dallas. Bob sat with his back to the wall. He didn't get up to shake hands when Luc and Danny approached the table. Frank avoided eye contact, keeping his focus on Bob.

"You know Danny, he's in town for the holidays, thought I'd have him tag along."

Bob showed no surprise, he trusted Danny. They were both vets and had a history. As it turned out he was the only one Bob trusted.

"No problem. Good to see you Danny. Do you still hang out at the Vet Center? I haven't been there in ages."

"On occasion."

Danny knew Bob from time spent at the VA regional Center. They were both veterans; Danny working on his ED, and Bob on his paranoid personality disorder. They both, as Bob put it, suffered from P-P disorders. It's the reason Bob sat in the restaurant with his back against the wall, he suspected others were out to deceive, or harm him. He was ever alert for the possibility someone may attack him any time and without reason. Danny figured Bob watched too many Inspector Clouseau movies.

"Grab a seat. You guys having lunch?" Bob had an empty plate in front of him.

"Just came from Denny's. I'll go for a beer though."

"What's your poison Luc?"

"Beers good, whatever's on draft." Luc sat down next to Frank. "How you doing buddy." Frank returned a slight smile of recognition.

After Bob ordered a round of drafts, and another limonada for Frank, who didn't drink alcohol due to his meds, he got right to the point of the meeting.

"I'm Frank's caregiver, he's been under my care for 10 years. He hasn't spoken since childhood, and has been diagnosed with a dependent personality disorder. I don't totally agree with the diagnosis, just my opinion. Bottom line he can't do anything on his own when it comes to making decisions, starting new tasks, working independently, and taking responsibility. He can only interact socially with a few people. It's why they hired me to be his companion.

"Any idea what caused this problem?" Luc looked at Frank, who gave no indication he agreed or disagreed with Bob's assessment, and Bob continued to talk about him as if he wasn't there.

"Don't know for sure Luc, the family speculates mercury poisoning when he was a kid. His mother was fifty when he was born, could have been part of it. Anyway, now he's an adult, and has graduated from university, which by the way took him 8 years, it's time to give him a shot at making a living. He doesn't need the money, his family is wealthy, but he can't play vegetable for the rest of his life."

Bob's bluntness surprised Luc. What little he knew of Frank from the bookstore, and his level of reading, didn't add up to him being a vegetable. Frank maintained his focus on the paperback in his hand, seemingly ignoring the conversation.

"What'd he graduate in, and if he can't speak, and has psychiatric problems, how'd he do it. It took me a long time and I'm functioning on all cylinders."

"Debatable Luc. The reason it took all those years is because you went into repairs more times than an Edsel."

Frank responded to Danny's comment with a smile and continued with his rundown on Frank.

"Frank graduated with a bachelor's degree in psychology. The new psychology building was named after Frank's father after a sizeable donation was left to the university in his will. Enough said. As to the offer; your friend Albert tells us you're unemployed since the bookstore turned into a freak show, we thought you might be interested. Frank's passion seems to be books, and the family thought a bookstore could be a good occupation for him to pursue. We're willing to fund the setup, whatever it takes, for a small paperback bookstore, maybe a paperback exchange, and you'd make it work for Frank. We'd negotiate a salary with the idea eventually the store covers whatever it amounts to. Your job, with Frank would be to find the place, stock it, and manage it."

"So Frank and I would be partners."

With this Frank fully joined the meeting turning away from Bob and focused on Luc.

"Yeh, so to speak. He'd be a silent partner."

Bob got a chuckle out of what he thought was a pun. Luc turned to his potential partner, and could see by the grin on Frank's face he was interested, and just might under his mop of hair be thinking it's a go. Luc wasn't sure who the caregiver was, and who the patient was. He was not ready to judge the book by its cover.

"You're into books, huh Frank? I am too. Let me think about it."

Danny downed the last of his beer. The meeting was over. He thought he'd put the icing on the cake.

"What are you and Frank doing New Year's Eve? Sallie and I have decided to spend the evening at La Cantina with Luc, and you're invited to join the party. We may be the only ones there to keep him awake. Besides it might be a good time to make him an offer he can't refuse.

J. T. DODDS

THIRTY-TWO

"Did you know Feliz Año Nuevo marks the day Jesús got his name and his dick clipped?"

Danny was nursing a beer, it was going to be a long night. Luc was standing behind the bar Danny and Sallie the only party goers sitting at the bar.

"You learn something new every day. I've been an ex-Catholic for years and somehow missed those tidbits of wisdom. Okay, here's one for you. If Sallie is wearing red underwear with yellow pee stains, what are her prospects for next year?"

"Easy one Luc; red if she wants love and passion, and yellow happiness and prosperity. It's why she ran away with me. Right hon?"

"I'm wearing white tonight *Hon*, and I believe in Mexico it's for hope, and you'd better hope you come through on the prosperity bit, I'm counting on it."

"I hope you can deliver Danny, I'm not having much luck lately, on all counts."

"Well if you're not wearing any underwear Luc, maybe I can start you out for the new year on a pleasurable footing."

"Thanks Sallie. We'll have to wait until the crowd dies out."

Luc told Francisco he'd keep La Cantina open for any downtown natives who wanted someplace to celebrate. Sitting at the bar looking at a quiet beginning to a new year, the endangered species act had just been passed in the States, and it didn't make the three of them feel any more comfortable about their prospects for the future. Leaving the door open and the jukebox blaring, by nine o'clock it had only attracted a sum total of two middle age Mexican couples, who brought their own tequila. Sallie scooped a handful of coin from the bar, slid off the stool and headed for the juke box. The Mexican couples at the table were playing conjunto norteño music non-stop since they came in, and during a lull, it was time for Sallie to jump in and temporarily change the channel with a little rock and country. FranknBob made their entrance to Freddy Fender's "Wasted Days and Wasted Nights." They stood in the doorway as if waiting for the maître d'cantina to show them to a table. Luc was on them.

"Happy New Year's, glad you could make it. There's a few tables left. What can I get you to drink?"

Bob scanned the all but empty cantina, pointed to the table closest to the back of the room, far enough away from the bar, and the small group of patrons, as not to have to communicate with either.

"Tecate if you got it. Limonada for Frank."

Bob acknowledge Danny at the bar as he passed by, and sat down at a table with his back against the wall. Frank, walking behind Bob, avoided the table, walked straight to the end of the bar, and sat on the stool closest to the baño. "The House of the Rising Sun" by the Animals tailgated Freddy Fender. Sallie stopped grinding with the jukebox, and sat back down at the bar. She squeezed Danny's thigh.

"Who are the social butterflies? The bald one seems to know you."

"He's Bob, the guy I told you wants Luc to open a bookstore for Frank, who doesn't talk."

Sallie leaned around Danny to have a look at Frank. "Seems to be a likeable guy. The strong silent type. I bet I can get a squeak out of him."

She got off her stool and danced over to Frank.

"Feliz Año Nuevo big guy." She put her hand on his thigh, reached up and kissed him on the cheek.

"Mexican custom. Welcome to the party."

She didn't get her squeak, even when she squeezed his thigh, but when she returned to her seat, she left underneath his shaggy mustache an acknowledged smile.

"Look at you Frank! You just sat down and already the women are making moves on you. It's going to be a fun party." Luc placed Frank's limonada on the bar in front of him.

He made a mental note, if they were going to be partners he'd check on his meds. Nobody should be taking meds that prevented one from imbibing on New Year's Eve. He also noted Frank's independent move to the bar.

After the Stones, Steppenwolf, and the Supremes one of the guys at the table beat Sallie to the music, and threw in a quarters worth of western, upping the ante. It was all good. While Luc carried on a one-sided conversation with Frank about books, Danny and Sallie moved over to Bob's table.

"This is quite the international gathering we have here Sallie. We got Mexicans at a table, a French Canadian behind the bar, and Bob McQueen here's a Brit."

"How'd you end up here Bob, you're a long way from the English Channel?"

Sallie cozied up to him on an adjacent chair. He stiffened.

"It's a long story, let's just say America needed me."

When it came to elaborating on personal information Bob paralleled Frank's inability to speak. Danny explained to Sallie what he knew about his not so forthcoming friend.

"Yeh, like Uncle Sam needed fodder for the war. After Bob got his mental health nursing clinical and theoretical credentials back in England, which may or may not be legit, he came to the States on a visitor's visa. It was the beginning of Vietnam, and if you wanted to stay over your visa limit you could join the army, and if you survived you could apply to be a legal alien. I think it's how it went down, right Bob?"

"I was one of lucky ones and survived. I may even go for citizenship someday, if I can figure out the benefit. I'll always keep my British passport, you never know when they'll go for another Boer War."

It was a tough sell getting Bob to open up, and during a brief spell in the norteño oomph-pah pah Sallie slipped away and arrived at the juke box together with her competition. She gleaned his handle was Gerardo and quickly discovered they had a lot in common. They loved to move to music. They took turns picking tunes, Carlos Santana's "Samba Pa Ti" replaced conjunto norteño. They were dancing to Proud Mary when Queen Vulvalita burst through the open door with her bare chested slave skipping behind on a leash tied to his black leather studded collar. She brought along behind them a garland entourage of leather and silk. She was on her way across the Stanton Street Bridge to welcome the New Year's in Ciudad Juarez, heard the music, peeked in, and spotted Luc. La Cantina, for a short time, became an oasis of *joie de vivre*, *alegría de vivir*, and joy of living all rolled into one

With a lot of coaching gestures Luc recruited a hesitant Frank to help him behind the bar and open beer bottles, and like a hyacinth opening to the morning sun, he blossomed in the moment. The Queen's entourage flew out the same way they flew in, a colorful superabundance of flesh and feathers on a mission, and left Angel and a lady friend standing in the doorway holding a Royal Dansk cookie tin. Danny, sitting at the bar was the first to spot them.

"The party's just begun Luc, the Magi has arrived bearing gifts and it's not gold, frankincense or myrrh." Danny put in an order for brownies and blow, and Angel came through.

"Let me introduce you to Verónica Ortiz."

Luc recognized the woman, she was Angel's date at Zipper's New Year's Eve party a year ago. His impression at first sight was the Mutt and Jeff comic strip characters, and the image hadn't changed. Verónica was head and shoulders taller, with a figure of a runway model.

"Congratulations you two. When's the big date?"

Luc was right in there with his favorite Mexican custom, kissing all the women you meet. After kisses all around Angel put the blue tin on the bar.

"I think Danny asked for chicken wings, but this should suffice. We'll set a date as soon as I can convince her padre and godparents I can afford Las Arras, the 13 gold coins we need for the wedding ceremony. You know I graduate at the end of this semester, the Chicano Studies Department has offered me a position."

"I guess he just has to figure out how to keep you happy and satisfied until then Verónica."

"He has his ways Danny." She squeezed Angel's butt.

"Calls for a toast everyone, and a brownie." Luc set up a round of tequila on the bar.

With an hour before the magic moment when time leaves the past behind and leaps into the future, even Bob was coached into dancing with Verónica. The Mexican couples who only spoke Spanish, now had an interpreter in Angel, and the marijuana brownies put food on the table. Gerardo, Sallie's Hispanic dance partner, upped the food ante by disappearing into the night and coming back with a shopping bag full of tamales. Along with Francisco's stock of bar snacks: a jar of pickled eggs, Frito chips, and peanuts, there was a midnight feast in the making. Drinking became secondary to the drugs and dancing, and although he exhibited the patience of Job, Frank soon tired of standing behind the bar waiting for someone to ask for a beer and returned to his roost on the bar stool. While Verónica and Sallie kept Bob busy gyrating around the jukebox Luc convinced Frank to eat a brownie, guessing it would have no effect on the meds he was on. Everyone stepped by Frank to get to the banos, and he became an object of a monologue for those coming in and out of the closet. His curiosity didn't visibly reach the level of inquisitiveness when two at time went in to snort a line of coke. He seemed to enjoy Sallie and Verónica teasing him, trying, with no luck, to get him out on the dance floor. He had company at the bar giving him moral support. Danny was not into frenetic dancing, and resisted all temptation to anything other than slow and easy. When the moment came to add another number to the year, and to one's destiny, Frank sipped the glass of champagne Verónica poured for him.

By 1 o'clock the two satiated native couples staggered off into the darkness, the dancers switched from frenetic-kinetic to bump and grind, and the door was closed. Luc and Frank sat around the table with Bob, it was time to talk business. Luc had typed a letter outlining his conditions for going forward with the bookstore, and he gave a copy to both of them.

"First off, as I said before, I'm game if you are. Frank. I've only known you for a short time, but I think we could work together. Bob, I doubt if I covered all the details, I'm not a lawyer or an accountant, and I'm not sure what all goes into running a business in Texas, but your lawyer will have it all covered."

They both began reading over the document.

"Let me just highlight a couple preferences for clarity. I'm not interested in a paperback exchange; yes it's a bookstore, but one with a limited audience which means a limited return on investment and time. Once you fill up the shelves, you're sitting on your thumbs waiting for someone to spend ten cents. If we're going for something Frank can be proud of and involved in, it's got to be a real bookstore."

"What do you call real? Something similar to your Colonel's bookstore?" Bob looked up from his reading.

"It took the Colonel years of collecting to get to what he had. No, real is one where you carry a variety of books for specific markets. At least if you want to be successful. I'm thinking somewhere around the University where the readers are. Students and Professors are forever looking for books, and bargains. There's a possible market in used textbooks. Anyway, it's what I'm looking at for Frank, and it's what I'd feel comfortable tackling. I put in questions about the financing, we'll need a startup balance in our account." Luc sat quietly while Bob continued reading.

Frank put it down right after Luc quit talking. He was either a quick study or not interested. When Bob finished he folded it in half, then a quarter, and put it in the jacket he had not taken off since he arrived. Luc couldn't read any expression on Bob's face. It came with the territory.

"What do you think Bob?"

"I'll run it by my people, and we'll see." Bob stood up, ready to go.

"How about you Frank, after all it's going to be your store?"

Frank gave it an enthusiastic thumbs up, both thumbs pumping iron. He had read it.

"Alright!" Luc stood up and pushed his chair back, "let's make it a prosperous New Year."

On their way out FranknBob got their hugs and kisses from Sallie and Verónica who then returned to the arms of their almost stationary companions while Elvis crooned, "Are You Lonesome Tonight" on the jukebox. Luc sat down at the bar, with a bottle of tequila for company.

THIRTY-THREE

Luc missed the University scene. It had been part of his life since he was discharged from the Army in 67. Without a goal, a mountain to climb, he'd come a long way to nowhere in particular. Before he learned to swim, he learned to dogpaddle. After all he'd been through he felt he was, as the band America's song went "In a Desert With No Name," dogpaddling around in circles in the desert of his mind.

La Cantina, as much as he was grateful to Francisco, was a hostel for his soul, and meant for a temporary stay on the way to where, at this juncture in his life, he had no idea. It was several weeks since he heard from FranknBob, and figured it was another might-a-been. When Francisco's father died, and he had to take up the duties of the patriarca, which meant Iglesia and familia on the Lord's Day. Luc came to the rescue. Unlike the Colonel's front door cowbells, there was nothing to announce anyone entering La Cantina. When Luc came out of the banos, Bob, the first customer of the day, was sitting

WHEN SOMEWHERE IS NEVER ENOUGH

at the bar.

"What's it take to get a beer around here?" Bob sounded surprisingly cheerful.

"Hi Bob. You don't know how hard it is getting decent help on Sundays. Mexican Catholics are hooked on this day of rest thing. You drink Tecate, if I recall, with all the fixins."

Luc walked around behind the bar, pulled out two cans from the cooler, squeezed a little lime around the top, and sprinkled them with salt. His not drinking while working fell by the wayside due to boredom, the devil may care's mistress.

"Thought I'd join you. You're it for the after church crowd. Salud! Where's your shadow Frank? I don't think I've ever seen you two not together."

"I do have a life. Frank's family are Evangelical Christians and it's all about God on Sundays. They insist Frank participates. Because I'm British I'm excused from the norms of religion. Momsy believes in only one God and he's Baptist. Besides on Sunday the horses are running at Sunland Park."

"Danny told me you were a hardboot, as he termed it, a horse racing enthusiast."

"Never miss a Sunday. I'll make this short and sweet, Momsy, who controls the purse strings says it's a go for whatever you want, and will have her lawyer draw up a partnership with you and Frank. They'll open a bank account in both your names with ten big ones as a start-up. You need to be available next Wednesday to sign the paperwork?"

Luc didn't expected this. He knew lots of things come your way, but few stick, it's the nature of life, the game of life trying to catch hold of what the wind blows by you. His hesitation was not for making a decision one way or the other, it was he had almost given in to another possibility of going nowhere.

"Is there a problem? You need time to think about it?" Bob caught the hesitation.

"What time and where?"

"Is it a deal?"

"It's a deal."

"I'll pick you up early Wednesday morning and we'll go to the lawyer, accountant, and bank. And by the way, thank Albert for convincing Momsy you can pull this off. You've won the Trifecta without going to the track, let's hope a little of that luck rubs off on me today.

Cuthbert J. Dingledine Jr. a dominating figure behind an oversized desk was a totally different species of lawyer than Mr. Franklin P. Peoples, Luc's divorce lawyer in Alpine, who shied away from making decisions. Mr. Dingledine Jr., spent all of fifteen minutes going over the paper work, the family's expectations, and getting the signatures, with Bob McQueen as the witness for the partnership. There was no room for discussion. A trip to the State National Bank where Frank's father, Judge Ronald B. Hightower had been a former chairman of the Board, to open up a business account and issue checks took all of another fifteen minutes to sign on the dotted line, with Bob again witnessing the procedures. Luc realized money talks, even if he had no clue on who was doing the talking. He got over it quickly with money in the bank, and faced with the first order of business. He went from neutral this time into first gear.

Sometimes the perfect location turns out to be the opposite. Guillermo's night club near the gates to Fort Bliss was ideal for tapping into hundreds of horny GIs. Horney GIs without a target won't get their marksmanship medal. The Colonel's bookstore, the only one in the downtown area, and within walking distance to the campus, should have been a natural. Trouble was the Colonel didn't market to the students, and an English language bookstore did little to entice the majority Hispanic community. Luc knew he wanted to be near the university. Close enough to feed into the demand for literature and used textbooks. Textbooks were tricky in as most publishers made money revising them every year forcing students to purchase the new volumes. To buy or not to buy was the critical difference in being viable or not viable. Buying and trading books would become the lifeblood, after location.

At first Luc searched for houses he could convert, with the idea of also making it a living space. He knew eventually the ladies would depart from the Brew House and he probably would be looking for another abode. Real Estate near the University was either not zoned commercial or used for student housing. Next was searching for a retail outlet, but nothing on the market came close to meeting his expectations or location. By the end of February he was getting desperate. The extent of FranknBob's participation up until now was to go with Luc and check out locations. With zero luck finding what he was looking for he needed help, and Professor Irving's wife Dolores came to the rescue.

Dolores had a background in Library Science and was a part-time real estate agent. She loved the idea of an off campus bookstore given the monopoly operating the university's bookstore, where students paid top dollar, and the variety consistently failed to match the demand. It was Dolores who came up with a potential solution, and one Luc would not have thought of. A defunct strip-mall with ample parking, four blocks from the gates of the University was vacant property, with a couple small outlets, and a former 7-11 convenience store. The store was a glass fronted shell of a space, which Luc passed over, assuming it was too large, and too expensive. The previous franchise renters when they left, stripped the inside bare. In this part of the word, anything not bolted down could be sold in Juarez. If there was any doubt about their ability to rent the space, it lasted about as long as it takes a cash register to ring in the money; the State National Bank held the mortgage on the property, and after being empty for more than a year, they were glad to see it back on the black side of their ledger. Hurdle number one was out of the way, next was to take a location and turn it into a bookstore.

THIRTY-FOUR

Professor Irving and Dolores, being Jewish had no house call to make Sunday morning. Frank was forgiven for missing the obligatory Baptist sermon on this special morning, and was dropped off by Bob on his way to the race track, along with four coffees from the donut shop conveniently located   around the corner. They were gathered together not to sing the praises of their particular deity but to take possession of the 7-11. Sitting on the floor in the middle of the store they watched Luc pace around with a clipboard in hand. This was Dolores's first meeting with Frank, and he triggered her motherly instincts, immediately taking him under her wing like the rare bird he was. The Professor recalled Frank sitting silently in the back of the classroom reading books, while attending one of his obligatory English Lit courses mandatory for all majors, and all sports teams.

"You're going to need an enclosed area for children's books, and a space the parents can drop their kids off while they peruse the shelves." Dolores was organizing the space the minute she had sat down.

"Great idea Dolores. Any suggestions Professor?"

Luc made a note to look for children's books in his daily searches. The only one's he had so far were three Shel Silverstein's, and a few children's classics.

Professor Irving was a reluctant participant at first, until Dolores cajoled him into remembering his roots. He carried a Doctors in Literature, and authored several books on major literary figures, including Luc's favorite Mark Twain. His passion for theater gave rise to directing student plays, and he donated a small but significant library of Samuel French plays to the new bookstore. The Professor was a natural when it came to books.

"If I could sit down and get to know a book, chances are I might buy it. What about an area one can sit back, relax, and maybe have a coffee while they get comfortable with the story. You've got plenty of room over where you're standing Luc."

The double glass door entrance divided the store into two thirds on the left and one third on the right. The left side was big enough for all the shelving they'd need. On the right Luc could picture a separate reading area, with comfortable arm chairs, pictures on one wall, coffee and music.

"Perfect Professor. We'll need music to sooth the troubled mind when choosing what to read."

"You catching all this buddy?"

Luc came over and sat down next to Frank who's head was spinning taking in the conversation. There was excitement in the air.

"We can't forget the books, right Frank. I think I've got an idea for shelving."

He was back on his feet again and mapping out rows of shelves. In his mind Luc was already staining shelves, and filling them with all those wonderful friends he left behind at the Colonel's. He was hyped and it was a good feeling to be a bookman again.

"I picture rows of shelves and all of them full. This is where we get busy Frank. We'll have fun scouring for books, but then I'll teach you how to catalogue and label them."

He plopped back down beside the Professor.

"You'll need more than Frank to put this together, you'll need a construction crew. I can probably find some volunteers in the Drama Department. We got some talented students working on sets. Dolores's book club will probably help."

The Professor was already committed to providing Luc with the course lists of reading requirements in the English Department, and was promising more from other departments.

"I think I can get Danny and Sallie to come down from the mountain on occasion. Miranda and Caledonia are still in school and are already excited about this. We'll do it. Right Frank." Frank gave it his thumbs up.

With the help of enthusiastic volunteers from the university; recruited by Professor Irving from the drama department, Miranda and Caledonia hustling the school of nursing, Angel donating a kilo of primo weed, classic rock on the second hand Hi Fi, and a rusty red coca cola cooler always full of cerveza, Frank's dream began to take shape. Having directed the construction of multiple productions on a shoe string budget at the university, the Professor came up with the brilliant idea of purchasing in Juarez folding closet doors, perfect in length and width for stacking books, and the store was abuzz with carpenters and painters.

Used books, soon purchased and donated were loosely piled on the tile floor, in boxes, and shopping bags, waiting for Frank to find a special spot on a bookshelf. Francisco's son Hector who had managed to beat the draft by staying in school, no longer had to worry about going off to war, or get a degree. He would finish the classes he wanted to take, and when it was over, assume the reins at La Cantina. Hector took over Luc's shifts, and was instrumental in recruiting the Hispanic students to help in putting the store together, adding a section for Spanish language books.

Come April, the convenience store was successfully converted, and contained all the attributes of a bookstore. Complete with a comfortable reading area utilized by everybody involved in the production as a second living room, a place to hang out, listen to music, smoke dope, and drink wine, all the while engaged in literary activities. What the bookstore flaunted in style, it still lacked in substance and name, and was not ready for prime time. Huge holes still needed to be filled in on the bookshelves. The lesson's Luc learned working for the Colonel were critical in moving everything along when it came to buying, pricing, and merchandizing. He dragged Frank along to every church bazar, estate sale, yard sale, attic and basement he could find in the one hundred and thirty square miles called El Paso. They were first in line on anyone advertising a hint of books for sale. He remembered scouring for books was analogous to panning for gold, where nuggets were few and far between and they were gold digging. Luc was discerning, but well aware empty shelves did not sell books. He would purchase everything he could in hopes when culling the herd it left him with enough books to fill the gaps.

Frank was a delight, up and at it early in the morning, meeting Luc for the day's adventure. Luc could tell Bob was not thrilled with having to drop him off at the bookstore, often in the predawn light. The pain of it was eased by the coffee shop nearby. Luc had learned the hard way the lessons of mold and mildew. The spores had taken root in his nostrils and he could smell it on a book just by getting close to it. Frank was a fast learner and somehow, beyond Luc's comprehension, he mastered the art of book scrounging by watching, listening, with an innate sense of what to look for. They communicated with each other out of shear love of the search, and bringing home the chickens to roost. At the rate they were collecting stock, they were still looking at the equivalent of a paperback bookstore by the time they planned to have the gala opening in May.

THIRTY-FIVE

The PEOPLES EMPORIUM, pumpkin, orange, and black sign spread from one side of the two story brick to the other, several feet above the doorway he had crossed through every day for months with the sole expectation he'd still be there today, until that is an unexpected twist of fate. He was returning to the now defunct bookstore on the chance the Colonel had not emptied his warehouse completely, and Luc might be able to pick up a few boxes of books. A young Hispanic woman guided him along the aisle, now stuffed with masks, makeup, black hats, and wigs, to the bottom of the Colonels' winding iron staircase.

"Senor Colonel, someone here to see you!" It was a clarion call, but tempered as to not disturb.

"Who is it?" A growl of annoyance.

"A Señor Luc, Colonel."

This was followed by a long silence.

"Send him up Angelita."

Luc had no idea what the Colonel might be feeling having gone AWOL on him. When he reached the top of the stairs and stepped into the Colonel's chamber, he felt he was stepping back in time. The Colonel, sitting behind his desk holding the phone to his ear, was exactly how Luc remembered leaving him for what he thought would be the last time. He gestured for Luc to take a seat. Nothing had changed, yet everything had. The shelves holding his prize collections were empty. On the shelf where once his treasured bullfighting volumes were on parade, Luc recognized the only one still there, laying on its back; *Or I'll Dress You In Mourning*, a biography by Larry Collins and Dominique Lapierre. Luc remembered reading about El Cordobés, preparing for his first meeting with the bulls of Spain, and saying to his sister Angelita, "Tonight I'll buy you a house, or I'll dress you in mourning." Among a catastrophe of paper and folders on his desk, there was the familiar half empty bottle of Johnnie Walker.

The Colonel hung up the phone without saying goodbye, and looked at Luc. "It's been a long time Corporal, is this business or pleasure?"

The familiarity of calling him Corporal made Luc feel a little less tense.

"I guess it's both sir. I don't know if you heard through the grapevine, I'm opening a bookstore close to the University and I thought maybe you might have some books leftover in your warehouse I could purchase. That's the business part, the pleasure is I wanted to thank you. Working for you gave me the ability to follow through on opening my own store, and the opportunity would not have come along had I not worked here under your mentorship." Luc was not prone to flattery but spoke from the heart.

The Colonel let this sink in. What had changed Luc noticed, was a bookman sitting behind the desk who no longer had that stern face he recalled from his first interview. Grey peppered his red hair, and the twist at the ends of his moustache had gone limp. He somehow looked older than Luc remembered him.

"I've heard rumors, it's a small town. I thought you had it in you to become a bookman. He thought about his role as a mentor, and realized, yes he did take the kid under his wing. He stood up, reached over and picked up two tumblers from the bookcase that once cradled Hemingway, and poured a shot of Johnny Walker into each.

"This calls for a toast. Salud! 'Second hand books are wild books, homeless books; they have come together in vast flocks of variegated feather, and have a charm which the domesticated volumes of the library lack.' That's Virginia Woolf speaking. Where's your store located again?" He sat back down.

"Couple blocks from the university. That's going to be my main market."

Luc sipped his whiskey. Something about the Colonel and the empty shelves in his lair now made him slip back into that uneasy feeling he had entering the store. The Colonel's informality was completely out of character. He had to ask the obvious.

"How's the Emporium business Colonel?"

"It has its moments, more profitable than selling used books, and thank goodness for the cheap shit from Japan. New Year's Eve, birthdays; the most profitable is the combination of Día de los Muertos and Halloween, from the end of October through the first week of November. Angelita, my manager, has been instrumental in attracting the Mexican community."

The Colonel mentioned profitability twice, this Luc thought was a long way from when he went on a minor tirade about the bookstore not being a supermarket or a shopping mall outlet. Luc was about to broach the subject again of buying any books he might have in the warehouse when Angelita announced another visitor.

"Señor Colonel, Jose is here."

The Colonel abruptly stood. "Tell Jose I'm coming down." He downed his shot of whiskey and put the glass back on the shelf. "Jose and I usually have lunch at the Bar Español. It used to be owned by Pepe, and famous for bringing in Flamenco dancers and guitarist from around the world. Pepe is gone, now it's a hangout for old bullfighters and aficionados."

"I know the place, I have good memories of going there when Pepe owned it. Great authentic Spanish food." He flashed on Kate. "I see you have only El Cordobés's biography left on the shelf from your Bullfight collection."

He didn't look at the shelf. "Yes, as Hemingway once said, 'there is no friend as loyal as a book.' Come, I'll show you what's left downstairs."

Luc remembered when he first entered the warehouse, books were piled on the floor, overflowed carton upon carton, and were crammed into precariously leaning bookcases that towered to the edge of unshaded light bulbs. It was, as he looked around, still a gold mine for the bibliomaniac.

"As you see Luc, I didn't have the heart, or the energy to get rid of all my books." His voice sounded as if it were coming from another room. "Take what you want Luc, take them all if you want, at no cost. I have no need for their company anymore. I'll tell Angelita you're coming to take them away."

He turned his back on them before they could make him change his mind, and left Luc standing alone. It was the only time the Colonel had called him by his first name. The words of Arthur Conan Doyle filled his thoughts, "The love of books is among the choicest gifts of the gods." The Colonel had squandered the gift for the almighty dollar, and it seemed to Luc, ended up empty handed. Luc saw the need to have something to go after, and it was more than just the love of finding a first edition Hemingway. There were two sides to change, that which gets left behind, and the uncertainty of the future. The Colonel was now hanging out with old matadors that had survived las plaza de toros, and he didn't want to end up there. He did not hesitate to look the gift horse in the mouth, and told Angelita, as he passed her standing behind the front desk, he would be by mañana to emancipate the warehouse.

Frank was not an idle bystander, he stuck to Luc like a bookmark in a book you keep on your nightstand. He was a big boy and hustled boxes with ease. He helped empty the Colonel's warehouse in one day, making multiple trips with Luc in the Volkswagen microbus. There was enough inventory to fill the empty boxcars in the store. Frank loved to stack books on shelves lining them up so the spines stood at attention, titles left faced, and he was gifted with the ability to alphabetize to perfection. The Colonel would have loved him. Once he mastered the plastic handheld Dymo Label Maker, and got the basics in the Dewy Decimal System from Dolores, there was nothing in the store free from his grip on the Dymo. He had no interest whatsoever in the business of running the bookstore, he was a truly silent partner. Luc thought there was more going on in teddy bear's head than Frank let on. He had read Einstein didn't speak until the age of four, and thought maybe Frank was just waiting for his time to shine.

It was Dolores who came up with a name for the store. It reminded her of Frank. She named it *Rare Bird Books*. She thought Frank truly was, as Juvenal phrased it describing a rare black swan, possibly a mute swan, as a 'rara avis.'

In Tall Cotton With Mark Twain

THIRTY-SIX

The two paragraph write up about the Grand Opening was buried in the back pages of the Herald Post. Luc would have seen better exposure if he followed the golden tit-for-tat rule, you get what you pay for, and he forgot to purchase an ad in the paper along with the announcement. He did, however, get a free write-up in the final semester edition of the Prospector. The student newspaper mentioned the grand opening adjacent to the headline—END OF SEMESTER BOOK BUY, generating a minor mob in the parking lot outside the double glass entrance to the bookstore. To appease the disappointed masses having to sell their used text books for a dime on the dollar, hotdogs and cans of Lone Star were available in the parking lot, while they lasted. Nobody bought a book that day, and it wasn't until mid-afternoon, when the register was empty, Luc shut the doors and hung up a closed sign. Frank, Bob, and the Irving's, accompanied by their daughter Samantha, slumped on the stuffed chairs and sofa in the reading room, too exhausted to celebrate. Luc popped a bottle of champagne and passed out glasses. Frank took one, it reminded him of New Years, and it was the beginning of a long friendship—he liked the bubbly.

By mid-May, students were getting the hell out of Dodge for the end of semester holiday's. The staff and teachers at the University were bogged down in marking papers, and booking their vacations. The summer students would dribble in once classes started but the walk in trade resembled the Colonel's, and Luc realized another golden rule of business—Timing. The summer slack gave Luc and Frank plenty of time to price and merchandize the store. In the parking lot they put on a small ceremony hanging the signage, officially making it public, 'RARE BIRD BOOKS,' was open for business. The old adage build it and they will come was on deferment until the fall semester. Frank was fine with it all, the bookstore was like a candy store for him, and he never had a problem finding something to do. Luc was bored out of his mind, and didn't have a way to escape the doldrums of a hot southwest summer outside of curtailing store hours, and hanging around La Cantina sipping tequila—until.

Professor Irving was offering a post-graduate course during the second summer semester on Mark Twain, his life, his works, and his times, and talked Luc into registering. It was scheduled for late afternoon MWF, and Frank could handle the store until Bob picked him up. Twain, was an old word meaning two, and a two hour course in the afternoon made for a safe passage from the temptations of boredom for the rest of the day. Luc was ahead of the game when it came to Samuel Clemens. An avid fan he had read all but a few of the novels, short stories, and essays on Professor Irving's class reading list. Rereading them was not a problem, and profitable. He was given an advanced copy of the book list, and he made sure Rare Bird Books carried as much as he could find of what was required for the nine students in the course.

The class was more than just a welcome break from the bookstore, the pleasure of studying his favorite author was made more enjoyable by the presence of one particular classmate, Susan Sundheim. Given 'Susy' was Mark Twain's beloved daughter, she cheerfully accepted the nickname Luc could not help but call her by. Susy was a graduate art student who Luc thought replicated her vocation, reminding him of Fra Filippo Lippi Madonna; delicate, pale skin, light eyes, and blonde hair, her softness in contrast with the intensity, and mystery she exuded. Luc learned that she had transferred from San Diego State after she fell in love with the desert on a vacation, and needed to capture it in paint. The Mark Twain course fulfilled a literary requirement she needed to eventually graduate with an M.A. What he didn't know is Luc fulfilled another requirement she missed since coming to El Paso, a companion to share the experience with.

Luc was back to study time at the Brew House, this time wine and pot were the only drugs of choice, and temperance the moderator of his appetite. The nine humans in the class, along with Professor Irving, who was considered a God, brought new life to a Brew House that had become for Luc, a seasonal hibernaculum of ghosts of parties past. Fridays became the day the Rare Bird hung CERRADO, a closed sign, on the front door. Besides the summer doldrums, when it came to retail most students treated studying on a Friday and Saturday as a mind-eating exercise, and returned to their natural state of insanity and dipsomania. The Brew House was a Friday afternoon destination for Twain lovers under the guise of a supplementary study class. Frank joined the class along with Professor Irving's daughter Samantha for what turned into an early evening soirée. By the end of July, with two weeks left in the course, Susy, who lived in student housing, was the only one who didn't go home at the end of Friday evening's soiree.

It was not by invitation on her or Luc's part, Professor Irving and classmates had wandered off into the night and left them sitting on lawn chairs on the back rooftop under a baldachin of stars. They had left the gathering, engrossed in conversation, to catch the last breath of sunset, and as night falls swiftly in the southwest they were wrapped in a mantle of silence just enjoying the peace, one of the benefits of the Brew House's isolation. Luc broke the silence when he heard the cars driving away.

"I think the class is over. Your ride might have left you to your own devices."

"Does that mean I'm in control, and can do what I want?"

"If that's the definition, by all means."

He turned in his chair and looked through the windows to see if anyone was still in the apartment.

"I guess they forgot about us. I can drive you back to the dorm."

"I'm in no hurry."

It was what he was hoping she'd say. For most of the summer program Luc did not have the opportunity to be alone with Susy, they were always a part of a conversation with other students and the Professor. He knew very little about her except that she was an art student and had lived in San Diego. She was Bahá'í, a follower of Bahá'u'lláh. Luc was wary of religion, up until now the word of God did not have a positive effect on his life and loves. She had never talked about Susan Sundheim, it was all Mark Twain, and he looked for an opportunity get to know her. This evening was a pleasant surprise and he took the lead.

"I could never figure out how to get you alone." He realized that wasn't quite what he wanted to say. "I mean we haven't had much of an opportunity to get to know each other."

He was stumbling and turned to Mark Twain for help.

"Twain wrote in his notebook that "A thing long expected takes the form of the unexpected when at last it comes."

"You should get an A in the Professor's class for that one. I'm glad we have become friends. It's such a perfect night, and this the perfect place to be. I suspect you might have planned this for our first rendezvous?"

"I spend a lot of time out here, it's a nice place to sit and meditate under the stars. It just got a whole lot nicer now that I know we're friends."

"Shall I put on some music, and maybe a doobie and a glass of wine?"

On a cautionary note he added, not wanting to break the spell.

I can always drive you home anytime you're ready."

"Sounds good to me."

While he was inside she thought about her present situation. It had been a long time since she had let the moment just be, come what may. Smoking weed, consuming wine were all against her religion, yet she tolerated social transgressions, for judging others also went against what Bahá'u'lláh, the founder of the Bahá'í Faith preached. She liked her new 'Susy' persona, enjoying her time with the first man she had ever felt comfortable enough with to let her guard down. She could leave San Diego behind for the present, knowing the future would catch up with her when she was strong enough to deal with her past.

Luc brought out a bottle of wine, and candles, placing them on the table between the two lawn chairs. He had found a classical station out of Dallas on the AM-FM radio Alejandro had left at the Brew House and they were playing Chopin. Susy was definitely in no hurry to leave. Dawn reached civil twilight when they abandoned the chairs, and he drove her back to the dorm, first stopping at Jaime's Hut for breakfast. Menudo was out, huevos rancheros was in. Luc waited in the dorm parking lot while Susy changed clothes and packed an overnight bag. They returned to the Brew House and came up for air only when he dropped her back at the dorm Monday morning, on his way to The Rare Bird. They had become 'good' friends.

At the end of August students and faculty swept back into El Paso like a sandstorm, and Luc was back into the bookstore fulltime. Students scoured the bookshelves leaving holes in Dewey's alphabet, forcing Luc and Frank back on the hunt for more used books. Professor Irving's daughter Samantha, one of a few women in the university's new MBA program, took a heightened interest in the Rare Bird. She was taking a course during the fall semester in Retailing Management, and thought volunteering in a bookstore would give her some valuable practical experience. Luc and Frank having zero tolerance for business management and accounting were overjoyed. Samantha was a trouper, maintaining control of the day to day tide of sales and finances. Starting the end of August the MBA program classes were scheduled in the evenings; allowing the students to advance their careers while maintaining their employment. She wasn't so much advancing a career as enjoying working alongside Frank, the strong, silent type, in an environment she had never experienced in her life. Samantha, encouraged by professional parents, was a straight 'A' student since kindergarten; and in the Rare Bird environment, for the first time in her twenty odd years of studious behavior, let her hair down. And Frank seemed to shine in her company.

For Luc it was boom time right through Labor Day weekend, which started on a Wednesday, and kept on truckin' until summer was a dusty memory. The Friday afternoon study group at the Brew house metamorphosed into a salon at the bookstore, at least an American version of a literary gathering, replete with local poets, artists, and musicians. The venue was soon expanded to Saturday evenings and The Rare Bird became an off campus destination. Kaitlin McCrery, a poet Luc first met at La

Cantina, organized readings; her partner George Logan, a professor teaching sculpture and pottery in the Art Department, along with Susy, brought in the art scene. Luc just sat back in his small kingdom of books he managed to scrounge out of the void in his life, and let it happen. He was a catalyst and enjoying every minute of what transpired in his life since he found a passion for books, and he found Susy.

THIRTY-SEVEN

Lacking Vivaldi's definitive four seasons El Paso danced along from one ranchero into another identified only by special occasions; for the Mexican population was their fiestas around saints and virgins, and for the Americanos, celebrating shopping days, and holidays from work. For both, November began the process of eating, drinking, and spending time and money on friends and family. As Francisco put it *barriga llena, corazón contento*, a time of full stomach, and happy heart. Luc got the bright idea of expanding his literary enclave by renting the vacant, narrow space next door to the Rare Bird and turning it into a student art gallery. It was his Thanksgiving gift to Susy, who along with George Logan's sculptures and pottery opened a whole new venue for the university scene. On Saturday nights it became the place to hang out, and the gallery was host to weekly local music talent. It also came with a student penchant for drugs and booze, all of which was brought to a dramatic halt when, with Christmas on the horizon, the week before became a Ho-Ho echo chamber of university students heading out of Dodge.

Much to Luc's chagrin, Susy was on the red eye to San Diego right after her last class to spend the holidays with her parents. Frank was roped into spending the time with family, while Samantha celebrated the Festival of Lights. If it hadn't been for Danny and Sallie showing up at the Brew House with a fresh cut popular New Mexico pinyon pine, Luc was looking at a lump of coal under a mesquite bush for Christmas. Luc left a string of Christmas lights in the shape of red chili peppers strung inside of the Rare Bird, and hung a sign: CERRADO PARA LAS HOLIDAYS on the double glass doors. Francisco escaped momentarily from the Feliz Navidad mayhem to let his son Hector spend Noche Buena at home, under the guise he needed to open La Cantina for those who had no place to go. Three, slightly intoxicated elves, Luc, Danny, and Sallie sat at the bar reminiscing about Christmas past and future— the present being self-evident.

"Tell me Francisco, how'd you manage to escape playing Santa Clause at home?"

Luc refilled his glass of tequila, and slid the bottle over to Danny.

"Tonight, Noche Buena is the Good Night for the familia, and they will be busy stuffing their faces, and drinking, all compliments of Papá Noél. The niños will not be expecting gifts until cinco de enero, when the Three Kings, Los Tres Reyes Magos come to visit. They will be busy celebrating Joseph and Mary finding a place for the birth of Jesus. No one will notice I'm not around. At midnight they will attend Mass, the Misa de Gallo, and after return to finish off all the food in mi casa, and all my tequila."

"Will Guillermo be there? Haven't seen or heard from him since Zipper closed."

"You are lucky Luc, we see him whenever there is a fiesta in the making." Francisco pointed to the 7 spike piñata hanging over the stage in the front of the cantina. "The piñata is an old tradition going back to the 15th century. The seven spikes are for the seven deadly sins. Guillermo represents one of them, Gluttony."

"He's a big boy, as I recall the telling. I suppose overindulgence could be deadly. Obesity and heart attacks go together. Something my Danny boy won't have to worry about, he eats like a chicken. And it's not my cooking."

"Chickens are voracious and will eat anything Sallie, even chicken. They don't get fat because someone will eat them first." Francisco topped up her glass.

"That's disgusting." Sallie sipped her tequila. "I didn't know they were cannibals. You're a barnyard scholar Francisco."

"Anyone know what the other spikes are all about? You're a Mic Luc, you probably have encountered one or two of those deadly sins, and if so how come you're not dead?"

"You're not a Christian Danny, so those spikes don't refer to you, except maybe Lust, one of the deadliest ones, and one that's non-denominational. I think the dead part means you're doomed to go to hell when you die, isn't that right Francisco?"

Francisco shrugged. "I am not happy with the clérigo who take my hard earned money and live the good life, giving me nothing in return except grief from mi esposa. She never lets up trying to get me into the church. I went when we married, when my niños were baptized and received their first communion. I went when they were married, and their niños were baptized, each time they take my money. When I die they will make money on my funeral. I want nothing to do with them."

He did, however, cover his ass just in case, with a large picture of the Virgin of Guadalupe on the wall behind the bar.

"So Lust is a sin. Did you know that Sallie? Learn

something new every day."

Sallie was sitting in between Danny and Luc. "At best you'd die happy. I don't think it's a sin unless you get Greedy. Isn't that right Luc."

"Sounds about right Sallie. And of course Danny would never get Greedy, another deadly sin, when you're holed up in a two room cabin all winter in the middle of nowhere, now would he?"

"If you call greedy never getting out of bed because there's two feet of snow outside your door, and it's fucking freezing, and what else are you going to do to stay warm, then I'm guilty."

"Mind you Danny's exaggerating, he does get up to feed the potbelly stove, or it could get deadly."

At over eight thousand feet above sea level, Cloudcroft was a pasture in the clouds in the Sacramento Mountains, and Danny and Sallie took root in the isolated community. They now managed to support themselves in several ways utilizing their combined nursing skills. Danny's hydroponic garden was providing medical and recreational weed to the locals.

"It sounds like you two have found a home in those mountains. Over the years I've seen a dusting of snow a few times in El Paso. I have no desire to expand that experience."

Francisco did not inhibit his consumption to the occasional toast, it was Noche Bueno and no one would notice he was un poco tipsy.

"I wish you the very best in the New Year and pray you have enough tequila to keep you warm. Let's toast your new life, Salud! When are you heading back to your casa in the frozen north?"

"We'll leave soon, possibly tomorrow. Danny has a garden to attend to, and the village will be celebrating New Years. You're invited Luc. You'd have to sleep in a sleeping bag on the couch. We only have a single bed and

Greedy here takes all of two thirds when he's not on top of me."

"Thanks Sallie, it's possible Susy will return after Christmas Day and I wouldn't want to miss her. Besides, I remember from the Brew House days you and Danny make too much noise, I'd never get any sleep."

"What do you think Sallie, sounds like Luc is getting serious with this Susy girl, and we haven't even met her. Another toast Francisco to the New Year, and love in the air."

Danny and Sallie stayed through the weekend and left Monday morning. Luc spent the week alone at the bookstore puttering around. He didn't take the Cerrado sign off the door, he assumed rightly no one would be around until after the four day holiday. Danny left a stash of his hydroponic weed, and along with classical music and books, there was little to do but wait and see if Joan of Arc would show up on her white steed. Mark Twain's daughter Susy was Twain's inspiration for the character in his novel *Personal Recollections of Joan of Arc*. It turned out to be like waiting for Papá Noél. When it came to romance Luc's brain, heart, and gut all got caught up in an imbroglio each vying for control all the while his emotions are on auto pilot. Twain called it; "When you fish for love, bait with your heart, not your brain."

Luc couldn't call it love, but it was the closest thing to romance he had experienced in a long time. They had been joined at the hip since the summer, and now upon reflection, his gut told him maybe he had missed something. Come to think of it, he didn't ever recall the word commitment entering their conversations. Samantha dropped by the store with an invitation. The Irving's were having a New Year's Eve party, Frank was going to attend, without Bob, and Luc was welcome to join them. He told her he was expecting Susy and was going to spend a quiet evening at the Brew House. New Year's Eve Luc closed up the store, stopped in at Jaime's Hut for a bowl of pozole, at the package store for a bottle of Sauza Blanco, and headed home. Angel dropped by New Year's Day on request. He had attended Albert's end of year party in the Barrio, and hadn't slept in two days. He left Luc with enough coke and smoke to kick start the new year. Having tempered his drug intake over the year, Angel's late Holiday package was like a gift from an anesthesiologist for when Luc emerged into the sunlight late Monday morning and headed for the Rare Bird, he had little recall of the first couple days of the new year. He had managed to put Susy aside, like a sore tooth he could numb with tequila, unsure if she would even show up for the semester.

Frank and Samantha had opened the bookstore and there was coffee and donuts ready for whoever dropped in. Samantha was at the front desk going over the course reading lists when Luc arrived.

"Feliz Navidad Luc. We thought we'd get a head start. Lot of students arriving this week. After New Year's Frank's been biting at the bit to get started. Speaking about biting at the bit, Bob dropped Frank off early, seems there's a problem at the racetrack, the seasons been interrupted by a horse virus outbreak and he's in a panic." Samantha paused, and looked Luc over. "Looks like you've had a rough holiday, you feeling alright?"

Luc hadn't shaved and was somewhat disheveled, both in mind and body.

"I'm okay Samantha, just a little rough around the edges. Where's Frank?"

"He's in the back pulling together the textbooks."

Luc walked to the back of the store and found him surrounded by a dozen boxes.

"Happy New Year's Frank. Did you have a good holiday?"

"Luc!" Frank sported a big grin under the mustache, and after a bear hug, stepped back.

Luc was shocked, it was the first time he ever heard Frank say a word. Samantha walked up behind Luc and put a hand on his shoulder.

"He also called me by my name on New Year's Eve. I think you'd call this a breakthrough.

THIRTY-EIGHT

For the first two weeks of the year the trio all but lived in the Rare Bird's nest. Bob would drag Frank home in the evenings, Samantha would take home the daily receipts, and Luc would crash in the reading room, smoke a couple numbers, listen to music, and wait for Susy. He'd head out to the Brew House late at night, or very early in the morning to shit, shower, and shave, grab breakfast at Denny's and then hit the bookstore. Frank and Samantha had left after a satisfying day of ending the first onslaught of students. It was the final Friday before classes started, Luc stood at the front door of the Rare Bird, dusk was hustling in as it does in the desert, chased by the phantom of a new moon. He just hung the Cerrado sign and was about to lock up when a baby blue Triumph TR250 pulled into the parking lot, and the driver cut the motor. It was far enough from the entrance to where Luc could not in the fading light make out the person behind the wheel. Susy got out of the driver's side and walked up to the bookstore entrance.

Her hug was one of hesitation, the touch of their cheeks a mere blush. Over her shoulder darkness cloaked the vehicle. He whispered in her ear.

"Welcome back."

He wanted to say I missed you, but something held him back. Susy straightened up and grasped both his hands.

"We need to talk Luc. Let's sit in the reading room."

Her voice was quiet and reserved at the best of times, this time it carried with it the attributes of confidence and determination. He let go and stepped back.

"Yes, of course. Come in. Do you want a tea, I've got the water on?"

"No thanks, there's a few things I have to attend to at school and can't stay long."

Words that put Luc on the defensive for what he quickly surmised—this was not going to be what he had envisioned. She noticed the holes in the shelves and the books littering every surface, the aftermath of a war of words.

"Looks like you've been busy."

"The first two weeks before the spring and fall semesters are the busiest times of the year. It's what the Colonel would have called it in his venery, a plenitude of students ravishing a cornucopia of words."

They sat in the two stuffed chairs they had occupied since the ending of the summer. Carol Lombard appeared out of nowhere and curled up beside Susy. It was the stray cat that adopted the bookstore shortly after it opened. Susy named her after the famous actress who was Baha'i.

"She missed you." It gave Luc an opportunity to say what he felt.

It gave Susy a focus avoiding eye contact with Luc. She tried, not always successfully, to avoid confronting situations that were emotionally difficult. It was one of the factors that caused her to flee to El Paso. She was leaving to go back to San Diego and didn't want to leave without an explanation, she felt she owed this to Luc, not wanting to hurt the man for whom she held a special place in her heart for the good times they shared, and for helping her accept who she was.

"I've never told you about what brought me here, besides the desire to paint the desert. That part was true. I need for you to understand where I'm at then and now."

She waited to continue while Luc stood up, and from a shelf beside him opened a half empty bottle of merlot and poured a glass. When he held up a glass for her, she declined. He knew what chapter this was, he had read the book to many times.

"You don't have to explain anything." He sat back down. "I'm confident whatever decisions you have made is where you need to be." He was trying to deflect possible bad news. "I only wish the best for you. You know that."

She knew he was covering his feelings. It was a defense mechanism she was well aware of, they had this in common.

"I need to explain...for me! My parents converted from Catholicism to follow the teachings of Bahá'u'lláh when I was in High School. I chose to follow Bahá'í because it offered a vision of one world as a unified field of harmony in balance with negative and positive energy... raised as a Catholic, something you're familiar with, I couldn't connect with the all-male trinity, and the inability to understand this God thing I felt was dismissive of our human potential. Women have a prominent role in Sufism and are treated as equals. Starting my junior year at San Diego State I met Sol, an assistant professor in the art department. Sol was a few years older than me, and a rare bird on faculty, being Mexican-American. By the end of the school year we were in love. That's when my life turned upside down."

Susy paused and focused on petting Carol Lombard.

"I'll take a sip of that wine now, if you don't mind. It's one of the things, as you know Bahá'u'lláh frowns on, as was chastity, but then again we all know perfection is hard to come by."

"Progressive improvement beats delayed perfection." He handed her a glass of wine and sat back down.

"Mark Twain, I suspect…progressive improvement began when I took that course and met you…I was running away from myself… I knew from my lover at San Diego State the art department here was excellent, and I love the desert, but the real reason for coming here was that both my parents, and my faith came into conflict with my heart. My parents were against Sol from the start. Bahá'u'lláh's teaching excluded premarital, extramarital, or homosexual intimacy, and Sol and I were intimate. For Bahá'í sexual expression is defined as exclusively between one man and one woman in marriage, and chastity rules.

"So you came here to sort it out. What changed that you can now return, and face your devils, if that's where this is heading?"

"The result of the conflict between my faith, my parents, and my feelings for Sol was guilt. Good old fashion Catholic guilt works for any religion. That was a hangover from my upbringing. I remember from our class another quote from Mark Twain: 'Grief can take care of itself, but to get the full value of a joy you must have somebody to divide it with.' I found you…and you were able to bring joy back into my life, and not feel guilty about enjoying it. You Luc, and Mark Twain, made it possible for me to go back to San Diego and feel good about what I believe in, and who I love."

Luc stood up and poured himself another wine. Susy had not touched hers. He knew there really was nowhere to go with this other than be okay with her coming to terms with the conflicts that forced her to doubt how beautiful both in spirit and mind she was.

"I'm happy for you Susy, or should I call you Susan now."

She wasn't put off by Luc's statement. It sounded distant, but she knew he must be hurting, for she cared for him, it was her nature, and she knew he cared for her. From the time he discharged from the Army, everything he got hold of slipped through his hands like melting ice cubes as soon as he assumed inevitability, or started to hold on tight. Every story had the same ending he was left standing alone on the platform as the train pulled away. He watched Susy open the door of the Triumph, wave goodbye, blow a kiss over the roof, before settling into the passenger seat. Before the car light went out, he caught a glimpse of Sol as she leaned over and kissed Susan.

THIRTY-NINE

With March break on the horizon it was vacation time for the Rare Bird, and the first one since the beginning of the spring semester. Business was steady, and profitable, enough to replenish the store on a regular basis, and it gave the three employees the impression they were making a living. Frank's father left him a sizeable inheritance, and what he collected from the bookstore was pocket change, enough for an occasional bottle of champagne which he took a liking to at the La Cantina New Year's Eve bash. Samantha was living at home working on her MBA on a scholarship, and since she did the payroll, she payed herself as a part-time employee. Luc was the only one who was paid full time out of the profits, which was more than enough to cover basics, and put a little aside. Given that the cost of living in Sun City was one of the lowest in the lower forty-nine, he was beginning to accumulate a little nest egg.

Aside from cost of living, hanging out in La Cantina every night after work, cut rate prices from Angel for one's poison, and a penchant for the working man's tequila, Luc's was not the lifestyle of a high roller. He tried to convince Hector to put in an eight ball table, to no avail.

Hector did not want the kind of clientele it would attract hanging out in La Cantina. Having taken over from his father and grandfather, he was going to carry on a tradition that had worked for decades. Through the end of what they call winter in the desert, now into spring, Luc had a marked loss of interest and pleasure in daily activities. He spent less time at the bookstore prioritizing searching for books, scouring garage sales, church bazaars, and moving sales. It was what he was good at, and it meant being able to withdraw from social situations and normal activities. The Rare Bird required time commitment and socialization; as the Colonel once stated the secret of selling books is to know how to entice a person into talking about what they are interested in, what their passion is—Luc lost the passion to engage.

There were times before he started working for the Colonel and found his passion, he sank into a dark hole devoid of answers. It had become a continuing pattern in his life, even at this stage where he seemed to have achieved his goals and reached a measure of self-generated success, he was in quicksand again, with the inability to make decisions and focus, preventing him from seeing how things could get better, or how he could improve the situation. As before, the exterior mechanism to cope with the emotional and mental pain he was going through did little to help the situation. Intellectually he understood, emotionally Susy had been a catalyst. He was back to tequila indulged sleep, and marijuana to anaesthetize the day. He was back to the devil driving and not knowing why, let alone where it would take him next. He felt akin to what he read about Sir Richard Burton who would run when the world closed in on him.

Any break in routine for Luc was both a blessing; relief from obligations and commitments of the bookstore, and a curse; too much time on his hands to think. Holing up in the Brew House left him alone with his self-destructive deep feelings of sadness. For whatever reason, and there were many; relationships that went south, dreams that didn't stand the weight of time, goals in hand that turned to sand; in his thirty years of sailing on troubled waters, whenever he anchored, the shore was sucked under his feet in an undertow of dead ends and promises. He was a poster boy for depression, and he could live with that, in the meantime he didn't have to like it, and there was always a means to escape, if only temporary, through drugs.

Luc knew it was the life he inherited, it's how it always was for as long as he remembered; where somewhere is never enough, and there is nowhere to go, but where the devil of a wind drives him.

FORTY

Professor Irving and Dolores took an interest in
Frank, and the budding relationship they observed he was
having with their daughter. Although interfaith marriage
was an underlying topic nothing was said, and once the
Irving's learned that Frank's father, the deceased Senator,
was Jewish, married to a gentile Momsy, the Evangelical
Matriarch, there was a reserved chair at their dinner table.
When it came to being Jewish, Frank just shrugged; he
didn't know the difference between a kreplach and a
kippah.

Frank took on the tasks that Luc first performed in
his apprenticeship with the Colonel: organizing,
merchandizing, dusting. With the encouragement of
Samantha he began helping customers locate what they
were looking for. His silence was not a problem when it
came to listening, and his confidence grew daily to the
point where he began to communicate verbally. First only
with Luc and Samantha in response to their constant praise
and prompting, where a struggled word or phrase, at first an
echo, turned into an acknowledgement, a thank you, a
request. With her volunteer experience teaching English as

WHEN SOMEWHERE IS NEVER ENOUGH

a second language in the community, and familiarity with melodic intonation therapy, Dolores was able to help Frank sing new words. She set aside a couple hours a week at the Rare Bird to work with him, and could be heard following him around the stacks singing words. They were an entertaining duo. Bob slowly faded into the woodwork, his services no longer needed, and when he won the Trifecta at Sunland Race Track he all but lived at the track.

With Susy out of the picture, Luc lost interest in the gallery. George and Kaitlin kept it going at odd hours, with little fanfare or promotion. It wasn't paying the rent and was targeted to close at the end of the semester. Truth would have it the bookstore wasn't paying Luc's rent either when it came to feeling good about himself. He had pulled off the road going nowhere onto a successful venture, but that was a repeat of many other road stops, self-perpetuating the results his expectations were it would all end poorly. He made it happen for Frank, and that was a good thing. Why it wasn't happening for him was lost in a fog of self-doubt and depression and a loss of interest in The Rare Bird.

When Luc was a no-show at the bookstore the Monday after March break, neither Frank nor Samantha were concerned. With mid-terms on the horizon, followed by Easter, on campus activity would grind to a halt, and they were looking at plenty of downtime lounging in the reading room. Tuesday was a no show as well, and since Luc never bothered to install a telephone at the Brew house they had no way to contact him. Wednesday when Dolores showed up at the bookstore to work with Frank on his speech, and no Luc, it was time to worry. Frank and Dolores decided to visit the Brew House, while Samantha held down the fort. Every day was market day at the El Paso Produce Company, Wednesday was the busiest, when restaurants and retail outlets across El Paso stocked up for the weekend. The gates were wide open giving them direct access to the Brew House. Frank pounded on Luc's front door for ten minutes with no luck. Frank turned to Dolores and tried to mime what he wanted to do. She knew what he was asking but feigned understanding.

"Use your words Frank."

He hesitated, and searched his mind. He pointed to the produce yard.

"ladder."

Then he stepped back and pointed to the space on the second floor at the rear of the house.

"Okay Frank, there's got to be a ladder long enough to reach up there somewhere in the produce market. Ask around, I'll keep trying the door."

She could have gone herself, but the teacher in her found every opportunity to force a few words out of Frank, and she knew he was concerned enough for Luc to accept the challenge. Eventually she saw him prop a ladder against the wall and climb up. She waited, trying the door handle, rapping her knuckles on the wooden door. A small crowd gathered in the driveway. Frank found Luc lying face down on the couch and tried to wake him up to no avail, until remembering Dolores, he ran downstairs to let her in. In the doorway Frank started gesturing toward the top of the stairs.

"Where's Luc, is he okay?"

She immediately realized that was a waste of time, barged past Frank, and up the stairs. She was not a woman to waste words. Entering the living room she noted the empty tequila bottle, joints in the ashtray, and a stale odor permeating the apartment. Kneeling down beside the couch she turned Luc on his side, and checked his pulse, and came to the conclusion he was just passed out. Frank had followed her into the room.

"He's okay Frank." She stood up and assessed the situation. "Why don't you open the windows and turn on the swamp cooler, while I make some coffee. If I can find any."

The kitchen was a disaster. She managed to find a jar of instant and put a kettle of water on the stove. Both Frank and Dolores were novices at dealing with the aftermath of a binge. She and her husband were social drinkers. The Professor liked his scotch, especially when directing a play, Dolores preferred her occasional Manischewitz. Frank got tipsy on a glass of champagne. After a lot of nudging and poking they helped Luc off the couch and into the kitchen. Seated around the table they watched as he laboriously sipped the cup of black Chock full o'Nuts Dolores made for him. The jar was labeled 'roasted since 1932,' Dolores wondered how long it was sitting in Luc's cupboard. They waited silently until he was on his third cup. Somehow they managed to sober him up enough to where they felt the worst might be over, at least for the moment.

"It looks to me Luc like you've got some issues you have to deal with... we were all worried about you...Frank here especially...What can we do to help you Luc?"

Dolores really didn't know where to go with this. She knew Luc had not been well, her interpretation of what her daughter described over the last couple months, and could only speculate on what might have brought him to this crisis.

Frank gestured towards Luc's cup.

"More."

He was close to having overdosed on caffeine. Not being a coffee drinker Dolores had put in a couple spoonfuls of a potent instant coffee in each cup.

"No thanks Frank." He pushed the coffee cup away. "Just water."

Luc folded his arms on the table and buried his head. He was embarrassed that they found him in this state. He still maintained a degree of pride even though he had given up on pretending to be in control of his life. He was a long way from the first step in AA, and guilt, even if he didn't clue in on the what for, playing heavy on his mind. The silent pall around the table continued, waiting for Luc to show positive signs that he'd joined the living. After an interminable time Dolores stood up and walked to the fridge. Motioning Frank to bring over the garbage can she began dumping anything that looked dead or dying. Frank followed suit going through the rooms and cleaning up. When Dolores finished washing a sink full of dirty dishes she sat down again at the table. She reached across and poked him to see if he was still alive.

"Looks like you need some help Luc. I'm afraid this goes beyond the skills I've developed as a Jewish mother." She waited as he straightened up. "You need to go sit in that tub of yours and soak." She called Frank over to the table. "Frank, can you stay with Luc while I go and figure out what to do next. Don't know where and don't know what, but the Professor might."

Frank spoke up.

"Yes." He sat down on the chair next to Luc. "I take care."

"Good boy, and don't let him near any alcohol or drugs. There are a half dozen eggs in the refrigerator, can you scramble them, and make sure he eats them. I'll pick up some groceries for when I return."

She walked around behind Luc and put her hands on his shoulders and kneaded.

"Hang in there son, we'll get you fixed up. The Rare Bird needs you, and so do we."

Turns out the Rare Bird didn't really need him during the mid-terms and Easter doldrums, Frank, Samantha, and Dolores had it covered. Professor Irving's solution was to call Danny, who said he was on his way. He'd take him back to the mountains with him to dry out. Until then Frank would stay at the Brew House with Luc, an arrangement Dolores made with Franks mother. Frank was thrilled, Luc was both his best friend, and mentor, and the first time he was on his own without Bob. The bookstore went on holiday hours and Samantha, after hanging the Cerrado sign, took over the domestic part at the Brew House: grocery shopping, cooking, and helping Luc pull it together. It was Easter week when Danny showed up to collect the body. He was not a stranger to Luc's addiction and depression having been through the Kate and Colette withdrawals, and then some. Nam was a quagmire of similar experiences, treating the wounded was equally physical and mental. There was no resistance from Luc, he had lost the will to struggle.

Frank and Samantha were holding hands watching from the gate of the Produce Market as they pulled away. Danny left the keys to the Brew House and Luc's vehicle with Samantha. They would be on I-10 in minutes, heading due west and would reach their destination by mid-afternoon. In spite of the stress around Luc's predicament, Frank and Samantha enjoyed each other's company and looked forward to playing house. For all their lives both of them had been under parental control, and since they met they were always subjected to public scrutiny. Easter falling on a Sunday, the Rare Bird was closed for the upcoming holiday weekend. Since Samantha had no obligations around the Resurrection, and Frank, not mentioning to Momsy Luc was no longer around, they had an excuse to skip the Easter Parade. They had the Brew House to themselves, and without weighing the consequences, decided to try on a little domestication.

FORTY-ONE

Instead of turning north on US 70 toward Cloudcroft Danny continued west on I-10, bypassing Las Cruces, and was several miles outside of Deming when his passenger, who had fallen asleep minutes after leaving the Brew house, woke up and rolled down the window. It was close to noon when Luc rejoined the living.

"Welcome to the living Luc, what gives with you and Easter? It was after another Easter, I can recall you took a dive, no a belly flop."

Luc held his head out the window, the morning desert air was in the low fifties and felt good on his face. The terrain was flat and peppered with creosote, the mountains barely above the horizon to the north east. It reminded him of his first trip to the Southwest heading for Alpine, and Big Bend State University. It didn't dawn on him they weren't heading toward Cloudcroft, he was a vacant passenger with nothing really sinking in for the last, he couldn't remember, long time. He caught a road sign flashing by: Exit US 180. He pulled back into his seat. His tongue scavenged his dry mouth for a drop of saliva.

"Have any water? Beer would be better."

"There's a thermos in the bag on the floor." Danny took the exit.

Luc pulled out the thermos, filled the plastic cup with black coffee, and continued staring out the window.

"This doesn't quite look like the long way to Cloudcroft. Not exactly the scenic route. Are we getting close?"

"We're a couple hours away from ground zero. Easter does seem like milestone doesn't it." Danny brought up the subject again.

"Maybe it's the rabbits." Luc's speech was as tired as a worn out joke.

"You mean like the Mad Hatter celebrating non-birthdays."

"Sort of...kind of...I don't know Danny. Had a rabbit as a pet when I was a kid. We lived in an apartment and my mom worked... It was my only friend... Can't remember its name... One day I came home from school, it was gone. Seems rabbits shit, and that didn't work in a small apartment. Mom replaced it with a budgie."

Luc topped up his coffee, and continued staring out the open window.

"Then there was the time I was a GI stationed near the Sacramental foothills while waiting to go overseas. A bunch of us bought 22 rifles and went rabbit hunting, for the fun of it. When I stood over the rabbit I killed, I threw my rifle down and never picked up a gun again, to this day."

"How did you get away with that in the Army?"

"I discovered I had developed a skill—avoidance. I was good at it...when the pain hits overload I can obfuscate or run away and hide...I guess I'm still good at it."

They passed a sign reading Silver City 52 Miles.

"This doesn't look like the way to Cloudcroft."

"You don't want to go to Cloudcroft, still a half foot of snow on the ground and freezing at night. You'd probably like it though being a Canuk. Besides Sallie gives massages during the day and it'd be a little crowded in a two room cottage. I got some free time until tourist season starts the end of June. Sallie can take care of the hydroponic garden until I get back."

"Okay, I give. We just passed a sign saying Gila Wilderness. Are we going camping?"

"Something like that. When I returned from Nam, like Alejandro I needed a break from so called civilization, a place to hole up for a couple months to get my head on straight. When I was a kid, my dad took me to the Gila Wilderness; no motorized vehicles are allowed, including bicycles. We found this Ghost Town on the edge of the wilderness, one of many, parked there and camped in the interior. Used to be gold and silver mining in the Mogollon Mountains, and the town had a reputation as one of the wildest in the West... I had a lot of ghosts to bring along when I ended up there...They were hard to shake."

Danny slipped into memory land and was silent for a long while. When he stored the memories he continued.

"Sallie and I visited Mogollon and stayed there for a week. There are a lot of vacant buildings, still livable. You're gonna like the hot springs, just have to keep your head out of the water, some springs contain amoebas, a form of meningitis that can enter the brain through you nose or ears and kill you."

"Sounds like a tourist destination. So tell me, why are we going there?"

"I figure you have a few ghosts hanging out in your baggage department you might need to detox from, and I don't think they're rabbits. Mogollon seems like a good place in the middle of nowhere to come to terms with them, and work off the drugs. You okay with that?"

Danny knew he was pushing the envelope. He also knew Luc's state of mind didn't leave much room for in-depth analysis of the situation. He didn't have a whole lot of buddies he could relate to that hadn't been killed in Nam, Luc was one of a few, and he knew if it was the other way around he'd be there for him. Luc leaned back in the seat, and closed his eyes. Caffeine was no match for his diet of barbiturates.

"You're driving."

It was mid-afternoon when Danny turned off NM 180 onto Bursum Road, drove through San Francisco River Valley and climbed for two miles on a 2,000 foot ascent to reach the ghost town of Mogollon. He nudged Luc awake as they approached. He drove slowly past the Silver Creek Inn, the stage stop, the theatre, church, saloon, general store, and a number of houses in various stages of dilapidation, giving Luc time to orient himself and take in the hundred year history. He pulled up on Main Street in front of a two story building, with a footbridge over a creek, leading to the front steps.

"Home sweet home Luc. What do you think, classic or what? I'm not sure but I think this is an original building, some of the other structures were built as part of a movie set for a spaghetti western called *My Name is Nobody*, starring Henry Fonda."

"Well it isn't Kerouac's Bixby Canyon cabin in Big Sur, but it's got something of a postcard quality."

Knowing Luc would kick in for supplies, Danny purchased enough to last for a couple weeks. Silver City was an hour and a half away when he needed to restock. Nights were cool at the high dry altitude, sleeping bags and a pot belly were enough to make it all livable. They occupied the second floor, one large room with a couple cots, table and chairs, and a sad looking lounge chair leaking its stuffing. The corner kitchen held a one tub sink with a pump, an icebox, dependent on the iceman coming to the still operational village store, and a two burner hot plate countertop stove. The room was lit by kerosene lamps and Danny brought along plenty of fuel for both the stove and the lamps. The first floor, having given up the ghost after the periodic flooding of Silver Creek was uninhabitable. The outhouse was a bit of trip, especially at night. It was indoor camping.

Initially Luc spent his days sitting on the second floor balcony watching an ever present light wind sweep the dust along Main Street. A dozen or so inhabitants lived in Mogollon year round, and occasionally one would emerge and stroll by, with just a nod of recognition in passing. To a man they all appeared as rough and ramshackled as their surroundings. The occasional small herd of Javelina trampled down the street, a white-nosed ring-tailed Coati cat slipped in and out of the neighboring buildings. Other than his ghosts, he was alone with his thoughts. He was aware he had an addictive personality, it's where he ran to when his minor depressions hit overload. The physical withdrawal symptoms from the cocaine were negligible, the psychological addiction was his to overcome. He hadn't been on the barbiturates long enough to have to put up with the nausea and sensory shit that comes from withdrawal. Danny knew of what he spoke, and brought him to a place where there was no escape, no running from the Devil, where he was forced to face his demons.

Mogollon at the base of Silver Creek Canyon, once provided a base for gold and silver mining in the mountains. Danny was content exploring the Canyon, panning for gold, and soaking up the decaying remains of a once vibrant community. He was well versed in the art of contentment with self, and left Luc on the upper deck battling with his ghosts. Toward the end of May Danny made one more trip to Silver City to stock up, this time just for Luc. He needed to return soon to Cloudcroft and prepare for tourist season. Luc finally came down off the balcony, and they hiked into the mountains to the hot springs on a regular basis. Physically, and mentally he seemed to have crossed the Rubicon, but expressed little interest in returning to El Paso. Danny planned to come back in the middle of June figuring a month more of isolation, no books, no music, no drugs, and no alcohol could be a motivating factor for Robinson Crusoe returning to civilization. Standing on the balcony looking over a deserted street Danny was packed and ready to go. He could make it to Cloudcroft in five hours, and was looking forward to curling up with Sallie. He did what he could for his friend, it was up to Luc now.

"Should be seeing some hardy tourists pretty soon. A good number of them will be on summer break from the universities and coming here for hiking and camping in the Mogollon Mountains, and you'll find them skinny dipping around the hot springs. You might have some company there. Nudity by the way is prohibited in the Gila, but no one was around giving out tickets when Sallie and I were here.

"I wouldn't think that would inhibit you and Sallie. Ever see a ranger in these parts?"

"It's a big wilderness, and I'm thinking they're few and far apart."

Danny was hesitant. Not out of fear that Luc would fall back down the rabbit hole, temptation was the least of his concerns in the middle of nowhere.

"You know buddy you're going to have to face the music sooner or later, no way around it. You got good people back there who care for you that are in limbo. I'm hoping when I get back you can head home to El Paso."

"I hear you loud and clear. I'm not there just yet, got a couple ghosts still hanging around I need to convince to take up residency here in Mogollon without me."

"Maybe some nubile students from the College of the Mines in El Paso will be hiking the hills now that schools out."

"I should be so lucky. Know what Onanism is?"

"Never heard of it."

"Mark Twain gave a talk which was suppressed, for years, titled *Some Thoughts on the Science of Onanism*, or masturbation. The final lines were 'If you must gamble your lives sexually, don't play a lone hand too much.' My hand is getting tired."

Danny speculated, as he drove down the mountain, Luc just might be on the road to recovery.

FORTY-TWO

It was Friday afternoon, the first day of July when Danny parked on Main Street. Luc was sitting on the balcony, one boot on the rail watching him as he pulled out an empty military issue field duffle bag from the van and dropped it in on the ground. He looked up and waved. He overstayed his trip to Cloudcroft and for good reason. He figured Luc would be no worse for wear and tear, and when Danny told him Sallie was pregnant, and he'd been preoccupied, it called for a toast. He brought along a bottle of Sauza just for the occasion. Sometimes tradition takes preference over addiction. Danny figured Luc would be dry enough, and if he wasn't, tequila would be the least of his troubles.

The conversation was all about Danny becoming a father, nothing about Luc's plans for the future. Danny did pick up on the fact that Luc was alert, calm, and ready to hit the road. Sallie had helped Danny overcome his erectile dysfunction caused by a pelvic injury, and the psychological trauma that followed. They sought help with a therapist living in Cloudcroft recommending exercises and behavioral activities, which Sallie was more than happy to oblige. One thing was certain, her man was never going back to living in his van. Luc, maybe for the first time in his life, was jealous. The celebration was short lived; Danny needed to get Luc back to the Brew House, and he needed to get home to his pregnant Sallie in Cloudcroft by Saturday. They left the room livable for the next inhabitants, and stuffed everything not edible into the duffle bag, the rest tossed outside for the critters.

It was dusk when they pulled off I-10 onto North Mesa, arriving at the Rare Bird parking lot after dark. Luc didn't have a key to the bookstore, nor did he really want to go inside, it was curiosity that made him have Danny stop by on the way to the Brew House. The sign in the window read closed for the Fourth of July holidays. There was a for rent sign in the art gallery window. Arriving at the Brew House the gate and door were unlocked; Danny had called Dolores before leaving Cloudcroft asking her open up. Frank and Samantha had enjoyed their domestic experience, and left it spotless. Inside the fridge they found a bag of tamales and a six pack of Coors. Saturday morning they ate breakfast at Jaime's Hut, the first time Luc tried menudo without a hangover. It cured him from trying it again. They drove to the downtown plaza, to Luc's bank. Danny sat in the van, anxious to hit the road, while Luc went inside. Returning to the van he walked around to the driver's side. Danny rolled down the window.

"This is where we say adios Danny. I think I'll stay downtown for a while, maybe drop into La Cantina. You need to get back to your momma."

"Sure I can't drop you somewhere?"

"I'm sure. Here's money for gas and the expenses you incurred, you're gonna need it, could be twins. I'll be forever grateful for your help, and your friendship."

Danny took the bills and squeezed Luc's hand. "Keep in touch buddy."

They had stayed up most of the night reminiscing over the years since meeting at Albert's Friday night get-together. A lot of water had gone under the bridge, and Danny's take was to leave well enough alone. He had parked his van, along with everything negative he used to drive around with. It was advice that Luc took to heart. He had left the ghosts wandering in the wilderness, and came to the realization there were plenty of good times, and friends he didn't have to leave behind no matter where the road took him. Alone in Mogollon he came to the conclusion he had choices, and what he pulled from his memory box, and what he chose to let lie was of his making.

Luc sat on a bench in the Plaza for hours and watched the downtown hub fill with life. This was Pam's favorite spot to come to and experience the Mexican heritage of El Paso. She introduced him to this world he came to love, and life just seemed to get in the way of his settling down here. He thought he'd walk up Stanton to the Rare Bird but stopped when he reached his old apartment Hotel Deux, next to St. Patrick's Cathedral. It was like an impenetrable wall of memories that if he tried to bypass would send him down the rabbit hole again; he turned, and made his way back to La Cantina.

"Where you bin amigo, my pop asks about you all the time?" Hector wiped off the clean bar top in front of Luc.

"On vacation in the mountains Hector. Sort of a sabbatical from life. I'll have a Modelo. How is Francisco doing?"

"Muy bien. Although he has a hard time keeping up with the nietos, they keep popping out of his daughters baskets."

"Awful quiet for a Saturday." Luc was the only one in the cantina."

"Summer time, plus it's a holiday weekend, people stay home to celebrate. It'll pick up soon, it's near siesta time, and the trabajadores will be in for lunch. Liquid lunch that is."

"Do Mexicans celebrate the fourth of July?"

"Mexicans celebrate every holiday and then some. You want a tequila?"

"I'll pass. The blue aguave and I haven't seen eye to eye lately. Just a cerveza."

On cue eight men entered the bar and grabbed a couple tables. Lunch time generally lasted from 2 to 4, and it kept Hector busy. All of the clientele brought their lunches. When the cantina cleared and Hector cleaned off the tables he pulled up a stool behind the bar.

"Looks like you've carried over the bartending gene from your father. Can I buy you a beer?"

"My father and my grandfather's gene I suppose. Thanks, but I don't drink."

"Good man. How's school?"

"I have enough credits that I can spend my last year part-time and maintain La Cantina. Getting married in August."

"No shit. Not waiting until you graduate?"

"Lupita is pregnant."

"Seems to be going around. Where will you live?"

"We haven't found a place yet we can afford, and we don't want to live with family, we want our own place."

"I might know of a place you'd like, real cheap. I'll let you know."

He left a good tip, knowing it'll be the only one Hector would see all day, and walked back to the Brew House.

FORTY-THREE

Impractical at the best of times Sunday morning was still a time for chilling out. It was his Catholic hangover. It wasn't actually a day of rest, chilling meant for Luc pacing over his options. He called Dolores to see if she could stop by the Brew House; his dialogue with himself was having trouble coming up with an end game. He knew, without a doubt, he could get the bookstore ready for the fall semester. Pricing, buying, merchandizing were the things a bookman knows to do. It was a conflict between his head and his heart with the soul as the referee. Dolores showed up with a bucket of Kentucky Fried Chicken.

"Figured you're going to need some fattening up after your forty-days and forty-nights in the wilderness."

After a bear hug she sat down at the kitchen table.

"How's the Professor doing? He's a short timer isn't he?"

"Retires at the end of this school year. I don't think he'll ever retire though. He's thinking of directing one last play, even talked about recruiting you. He never did direct Waiting for Godot, after you couldn't take a part. He could arrange it if you're interested, as a graduate student that is."

Luc let that one fly by. Working on an Master's was no longer an option.

"You must be looking forward to having him home all the time."

"He's underfoot all the time anyway, only teaches one class a semester. I get to escape going to the Rare Bird. With my library experience, I can help Frank keep it organized, and he's progressing with speech."

"Tell me about Frank and Samantha, are they holding up with me not being around?"

"At first it wasn't a problem, business was slow and steady. Students coming into sell their books before and after finals got a little out of hand. They put a sign up saying no more textbooks required. The Professor helped, but that's where your expertise was really missed. Stock has been depleted, and they don't have the knowledge base to buy and price, especially the hardbacks and oversize books. Paperbacks are no problem."

Dolores didn't know how Luc would take what she was going to say, and when he didn't comment on what she was telling him so far she laid out the ideas Frank and Samantha were thinking about, in the off chance he wasn't returning to Rare Books. Luc sensed her hesitation.

"Frank's dream was a paperback bookstore. That was the catalyst to all this. I'm the one who wanted to go full lit, and I convinced the powers to be to fund it."

"I think it still is. Samantha has some ideas on that she'll want to go over with you. I don't think you know this but while you were away they got engaged. The plan to marry after she completes her MBA. Frank's mother is delighted."

"That's great. I suspect Bob's completely out of the picture."

"Ever since he won the trifecta we haven't seen hide nor hair of him."

"How does Samantha see this all unfolding?"

"Possibly dividing the space into two separate, smaller, yet complimentary entities; one the paperback exchange, and the other a more upscale area with hardbacks, textbooks etc., that you'd manage. What do you think Luc?"

"It's got a lot of possibilities Dolores. Let me digest how we might go about it."

She stood up ready to leave.

"I have some last minute shopping to do. We're having a few people over for the traditional Fourth of July barbecue. If you'd like to join us tomorrow you be more than welcome. The Professor would love to see you. Frank and Samantha will be there. We've all been waiting anxiously for your recovery."

Another bear hug, and Luc was left with only one option. It took him what was left of Sunday and most of Monday morning to get his act together, and jot down a plan of action for the bookstore. He dropped off the van at the nearby gas station, to have the mechanic Sergio give it a quick safety check, top up everything, and have a kid wash it down. There was nothing in the Brew House he needed to put a stamp on. When they delivered the microbus he loaded his typewriter and Danny's duffle bag, still unopened from Mogollon, in the back of the van, and headed to The Rare Bird, stopping first at La Cantina. Instead of Hector, Francisco came in to open up on the holiday. Francisco knew there would be no customers, but it was his opportunity to let Hector celebrate with familia, and for him to escape the chaos.

"Hola Francisco. It's been a long time." Luc pulled up a stool.

"Hector told me you were around. He hadn't seen you for many months. All is well?"

"As well as could be I suppose. I'm only stopping in for a moment."

"How's your buddy Danny? Angel tells me he's moved to New Mexico and not returning. I'll miss his van parked out in front. You can park yours there any time."

"Moved and soon to be a father."

"No!" This was great news for Francisco who had evolved into loving time with his nietos. "That calls for a toast."

He retrieved a bottle of tequila from under the bar.

"Just one Francisco, I'm on a mission."

"Salud! For Danny."

Francisco downed his shot. Luc let his sit on the bar.

"What is this mission you are on Luc?"

"Hector tells me he is getting married and has not found a place to live yet that he can afford." Luc took an envelope out of his jacket pocket and put it on the counter. "You know the Brew House, if he is interested here is the key, it's furnished, and the rent is paid through August. The name of the landlord and phone number are in the envelope. Danny will have no problem calling and giving Hector a reference. If he doesn't want it could you please call the landlord to pick up the key."

"Are you heading back to where, Canada? That would be a stretch for that Volkswagen I sold you."

"No, I'll be heading west this time. It should get me as far as the ocean...after that, the good Lord willing, it'll carry me home."

Luc stepped down from his stool and raised his glass.

"Salud! To Danny, and to you Francisco, I hope our paths will cross again."

Luc didn't answer Francisco's question, asking what mission he was on, it was complicated, and as he walked out of the cantina Francisco poured himself another shot and called out to him.

"*Las piedras rodando se encuentan.* Adios Luc.

He knew rolling stones might meet up again. He wasn't sure if Luc would ever pass this way again.

FORTY-FOUR

The Rare Bird's nest was partially empty, not in tatters, but a little threadbare on many of the shelves. Luc kept the lights off, it was bright enough with the sunlight coming through the front windows. He noted a new sign prominently displayed at the front desk outlining the guidelines for paperback, and hardback exchanges. Not having read anything over the last half a year he wandered through the stacks and picked out a few books to take with him: *Mr. Goodbar, Something Happened*, and "*Humboldt's Gift*". He proceeded to the reading room where Carol Lombard was curled up on one of the stuffed chairs. He pictured Susy sitting beside her. He check her food dish, and gave her fresh water before opening the Hi Fi and skimming through the albums. He put on the Moody Blues *Days of Future Passed*. On the shelf above the stereo Luc removed one of the volumes of the Books in Print and retrieved the stash of weed he put behind it months ago. He rolled a number, sat back in his favorite chair, and reflected on the decision he had come to.

He had achieved a couple letters in the alphabet he'd been working on forever, discovered a passion he was good at, reached a modicum of success with a Rare Bird that couldn't be cadged, put a few lines on a one page resume, fought back, and for the moment knocked the devil of addiction off his shoulder. Now in his thirties the so called progress he made in his journey resounded in sync with The Stone's, "Can't Get No Satisfaction," and after what seemed like a lifetime in El Paso, Texas, there was just too much baggage weighing him down, and this somewhere he kept returning to was never enough. He felt good about his decision that he needed to find some place, as Danny tagged it, he could hang the hat he never wore.

Dusk was fast approaching when he got up the courage to make his move. He turned off the music, picked up Carol Lombard and gave her a hug, causing her to jump out of his arms and head for the stacks. He left money to pay for the books he was taking with him and a note outlining a plan of action for the bookstore on the front desk for his now not so silent partner. He locked the front door behind him and never looked back. He could almost hear the bells over the Colonel's door as he walked across the parking lot.

Frank and Samantha

Francisco left me with a Mexican saying
stones keep rolling and may cross paths again

let the Rare Bird fly away
rent the gallery next store
make it Frank's paperback exchange

You never know,
I may pass by this way someday
looking for the perfect paperback cover

Adios Amigos

Heading west on I-10 Luc planned on following the sunset until it ended on the shores of the Pacific, and check in with Lee and Alejandro. Before crossing the Texas, New Mexico border he veered off the interstate at Trans Mountain Road, and pulled up. He thought about driving up to Franklin Mountain State Park where Pam had taken him to catch the sunset before she left, then changed his mind when he saw a streak of turquoise in the setting sun. Pam had told him it was a sign that harbored good luck and fortune. It was the universe telling him to stay the course—he was on the right path. He pulled back onto I-10. It was a new moon, and his guiding light was the tail end of an 18 wheeler.

THE END

ABOUT THE AUTHOR

John Thomas Dodds has-published a collection of 15 volumes, of poetry on prominent online platforms. His repertoire includes two enchanting children's books composed in verse, *A Sneaky Twitch of an Itch* and *The Journey Home*, as well as a poignant compilation of essays and poetry centered on the subject of aging, titled *Comes A Time*.

Permanently residing in the tranquil village of Ajijic in Jalisco, Mexico, John shares his life with his wife, Candis, and a cherished clowder of furry companions. Under the pen name J.T. Dodds, he has crafted five novels online: a trilogy *To Each Their Own Goodbye*, consisting of Book 1: *Anywhere Except Yesterday*, "Book 2: *A Long Way From Nowhere*, and Book 3: *When Tomorrow Is Never Enough*. Additionally, John has penned two standalone novels titled *If You Are Born To Be A Tamale,* and *Wanting To Breathe Her In.*

Milton Keynes UK
Ingram Content Group UK Ltd.
UKHW041822211123
432980UK00001BB/140